TRIALS OF *Destiny*

BARBARA SULLIVAN-NELSON

XULON ELITE

Xulon Press Elite
2301 Lucien Way #415
Maitland, FL 32751
407.339.4217
www.xulonpress.com

Cover Design by: Susan Leslie

Paperback ISBN-13: 978-1-66287-312-6
Ebook ISBN-13: 978-1-66287-313-3

Trials of *Destiny*

One

Shelby shuddered. **A** sudden downpour of rain drenched her clothing, causing it to cling to her like limpid paper. Her arms and legs tingled from cold. A painful stinging imposed upon her face. Mystical cries groaned from the wild. She was fearful of dangerous beasts. She had forced her way down a dark country road in search of a farmhouse after her truck plunged hard into a muddy trench. No farmhouses were in sight. No one in the fields, and no passers-by. She prayed for a passing vehicle and someone to rescue her.

Her mind shifted to her childhood when in the second grade she had run out of school, stumbled, and fell over a stray dog. No one noticed her when the school bus pulled away, leaving her alone to wander out onto a country road blinded by wind and rain. When she failed to exit the school bus at her home, her parents called the school, but no Shelby. Frantic with fear, her dad called the police, and at once, an intense search of the area began with law enforcement and numerous volunteers. Hours later, her father found her three miles from home alongside the lonely road, huddled on top of a heap of leafy branches, and fast asleep. He claimed it was not a stroke of luck when a flash of lightning directed him to the form of his young daughter wrapped in a pink rain jacket, but an attendant spirit, an angel, sent by God to watch over her.

Now, years later, in the twilight hours on an evening in June, Shelby, a twenty-seven-year-old professional journalist, again, stumbled alone, isolated by misfortune. The desirable warm climate that embraced Kentucky during the summer months, plummeted to discomforting temperatures during a downpour of rain. Shelby flinched at electrifying sounds from the depths of a dense forest, closed her eyes, and urgently implored her guardian angel to reappear. Suddenly, as if an answer to her prayer, a faint shadow of indirect light bounced downhill from over a rise and intermittently flashed a glow of illumination upon the road. Shelby ran down the center of the graveled path, impaired, over time by trucks traveling back and forth from a distant coal mine. She soon faced beams of piercing brightness, breathed a sigh of relief, and frantically waved her arms toward the approaching vehicle. Her ominous nightmare was over.

"I will send someone out tomorrow to pull my truck out of the ditch", Shelby mumbled, grateful she would soon be safely on her way home. She prepared to explain to the driver what had happened with her vehicle when her expectation of good fortune sank as if swallowed by vast fathoms of seawater. Two jeering men dressed in fatigues jumped out both doors of the old truck, yelled obscenities, and as two starving, mad dogs in lust for food, readied for attack.

Shelby bolted as if shot by a crossbow and ran from the condemning headlights. She crouched in recoil behind the tumbledown, dilapidated truck that idled like thunder, and wildly determined an escape route.

Two

On a Friday afternoon in June of 2012, Shelby had intuitively diverted from her daily routine after work, rush home to finish reading a novel, or to write an article of importance for the newspaper. Instead, she set out to explore the countryside. After justly learning the ropes in her new position at the DAILY RECORD, a paper in a rural county in Eastern Kentucky, she was anxious to familiarize herself with her new surroundings.

Her friends and former co-workers had concernedly questioned Shelby's sanity when she chose to leave the bustling city of Chicago where her notable success as chief reporter for the TRIBUNE offered favorable opportunities for her future.

"You can't take the country out of a hick," Shelby jokingly told her friends.

Her instinctual drive had convinced her a rural, peaceful town would support the familiarity and appreciation of a smaller, unceremonious community. Childhood experiences on a farm with her parents encouraged her to remain firm with the decision for change. Also, the move presented a safer environment to Shelby who wrote topical news stories while reporting for the TRIBUNE, sometimes describing loathsome criminals. She had received several pernicious threats after her documented reports on known crime figures. Shelby's parents, Janet, and John Evans, both teachers at a rural high school in Indiana where their daughter grew up, supported her decision. They had been privy to the threats against their daughter and feared for her safety in Chicago where crime figures were known to have dominated sections of the city, and where violence was prevalent.

Shelby's deeply rooted passion for developmental training of children grew her interest in community service in rural areas. Due to statistics, she found numerous children had failed to develop a lust for knowledge in high school and had dropped out of school at an increased rate in rural areas.

In researching selective job opportunities in Midwestern States, Shelby sought employment close to her parent's home in Indiana. After finding limited prospects in Indiana, she became inspired by a county in Kentucky, and the background of Sam Shoney, the editor of a popular newspaper with an extraordinary appeal to the public, The RECORD. The newspaper printed syndicated documentaries, articles, and world news items from around the globe in addition to local news. The newspaper was of interest to many outlying counties, with a substantial number of subscriptions.

Shoney's education of a variety of subjects unfolded an expansion of knowledge through his editorials. He had also left a large city where his co-workers had well stated his outstanding prominence. After having met with Shoney a couple of times, Shelby decided where she wanted to work and live and accepted his offer of employment. She had impressed Shoney by her background and personality. He recognized her good sense of leadership as well and offered she might contribute a purposeful difference to benefit the community. He discussed with her his concerns of residents who lacked in broader spectrums of education despite efforts of town leadership. He surmised that Shelby's, goals, and ideas, combined with the town council's expertise, would be an asset to the townspeople. He suggested that with her drive and credentials, aside from her journalism career, she might acquaint herself with members of the school board and consider teaching at the high school. The prospect of teaching a journalism class elevated her interest as well.

Three

Once settled in, Shelby began to study the history of the town in which she settled and of the State of Kentucky. She acquainted herself with members of the community and set out to learn how a small village had developed into a town. She discovered the town had acquired its name of Poa from the official scientific name of Kentucky Bluegrass, Poa Pratensis. The thick sod from Europe and Asia in the 1800s had inspired North American settlers who brought the grass to the United States and distributed and planted it in numerous pastures of Kentucky. Kentucky was then descriptively dubbed the Bluegrass State. Residents found the perennial herb was nourishing for animals and withstood a lot of trampling, rendering it practicable for lawns and golf courses.

The welcome sign in the town square boasted a population of 8,528. The town had a quiet and unchanging character. Many inhabitants either toiled their lands as farmers or labored in the coal mine. Others worked in the schools, government offices, or commuted to work in nearby counties. It seemed as if the town's development had suspended in growth except for a few apartment building constructions in progress.

Two doctors in the small town operated a medical clinic equipped with hospital beds and equipment in preparation for minor surgeries and childbirth if necessary. A dental office provided care to those patients who preferred not to travel the fifty-mile trip to Richmond.

Judge Morley, and two tax attorneys, and Shoney, who served the town as mayor as well as editor of the newspaper, occupied offices on the second floor of the two-story Fiscal building on Main Street. Shoney rarely used his downtown office unless calling together a council meeting. He spent most working hours at the newspaper office. The Fiscal building also housed offices for local government records and an accountant. Around the corner from Main and Magnolia streets, obscured between clusters of low hanging, weeping willows, stood an old one-story jailhouse. The century-old building, with vertical windows too narrow for anyone to slip through, was built in 1908 by first settlers, denoted by a carved inscription in the stone structure. An original hitching post at the front side of the building, preserved as a landmark, signified an historical fact. At the rear of the original building, prisoners watched passers-by through barred windows from inside a more modern jailhouse, a brick, free-standing, two-story building. The prisoners, most of whom were repeat offenders jailed for petty crimes such as pilfering or disorderly conduct, were released in short order. Severe crimes rarely occurred in the quiet town but were dealt with according to the significance of violence.

Quaint shops interspersed along Main, Elm, and Magnolia Streets where local merchants offered: antiques, trinkets, arts and crafts, memorabilia, handmade quilts from a clothing and fabric shop, hand-crafted birdhouses, and various items from Woody's woodworking shop. Delectable homemade cakes and loaves of bread from Bonnie's Bakery, widely known to surrounding areas, satisfied taste buds of residents as well as frequent visitors. In spring, various flowering dogwood trees, redwood trees, and shrubs created attractive settings along Main and Magnolia Streets.

Shelby studied the history of Kentucky, how the name 'Kentucky' derived from a Cherokee Indian word with dual meanings of "Land of Tomorrow" and "Meadowland". She remembered how the State borders between the north and south, and the Ohio River forms the entire northern boundary of the State. The civil war battles fought in Kentucky were of interest to her, and how, at the city of Richmond, Confederate soldiers won a contest in 1862. She read that both the North and South lost significantly at Perryville, and Union soldiers had retreated into Tennessee. She reviewed the conflicts of slavery and how the North and South suffered during, and after the Civil War. And during World War Two, Kentucky factories developed war materials, changing the State from an agricultural to an industrial economy. The coal industry brought revenue to Kentucky in the 1970s despite powerful coal companies whose owners blasted the ground, destroyed trees, and bulldozed away mountainsides by strip-mining. The difference between traditional mining and deep mining, as opposed to strip mining used in the 1970s, fascinated Shelby. She discovered that a black sludge called slurry, a toxic substance formed by powdered coal and mixed with water, created hidden ponds, and contaminated the land. She read the criminal violence and corruption by employers who forced their employees to sign a contract called the "Yellow Dog Contract", a declaration not to join a labor union. The agreements became unenforceable in 1932 through the "Norris-La Guardia Bill", which prevented employers from suing their employees in Federal court for breaking the "Yellow-Dog Contract". Shelby found which coal-producing counties in Kentucky and Tennessee continued to operate where the Federal Government permitted.

The history of horse racing excited her curiosity, how its popularity increased after the Civil War when farmers were encouraged to raise thoroughbreds. She remembered, as a child, visiting Frankfort, the Capital of Kentucky since 1793, and horse farms in Lexington, Kentucky, and walking through the famous horse park in Lexington. "Man O' War", the most famous horse during the 20th century, was buried in his entirety at the park. Secretariat, another famous horse, was placed, whole, in a casket lined with orange silk cloth and buried at an equine farm in Paris, Kentucky. The horse had won the Triple Crown: The Kentucky Derby, Preakness Stakes, and Belmont Stakes in 1973. Cremating a dead horse's body was traditional, although, at times, the head, heart, and hooves were buried, signifying intelligence, spirit, and speed.

Shelby scheduled time to visit popular tourist attractions in Kentucky, such as Mammoth Cave and Cumberland Falls. When she had time, she visited famous distilleries, since the State was a leading producer of bourbon whiskey. She particularly enjoyed Churchill Downs Museum in Louisville where she toured the grounds and stables at the track. She traveled another fifty miles to Fort Knox, south of downtown Louisville, where the storing of gold reserves in the United States Mint was a principal point of interest. The army had created its first military armored force at Fort Knox in 1940. The famous Patton Museum of armor displays military vehicles, equipment, and artifacts at Fort Knox.

Closer to home, Shelby explored shopping centers with larger food chain stores that offered a variety amenities not available in her town. She put to her memory the locations of hospitals and government offices, conveniently located in Richmond. There was so much to learn and inspiring stories to remember about the State she chose as her home.

Four

After several weeks at her new job, Shelby reminded herself she had not taken time to explore the county where she lived and set out on a Friday afternoon after work to tour her more immediate surroundings. She passed through shaded streets at a casual site-seeing rate of speed. She smiled and waved to a group of elementary-age children playing catch on Elm Street, and to a young couple wearing bluejeaned overalls getting into a spotted green jeep on Main Street, before she decisively ventured out of the city limits.

Shelby, anxious to explore the rural countryside and become acquainted with its people, drove north through the rural district. She drove by a stretch of open park-like land she suspected was a neglected golf course. She passed cornfields, and crops of soy and slowed for a better view of a horse farm with a training track, suitable for thoroughbreds. Colorful blue and yellow wildflowers cascaded exquisite color along black fences. A sweet fragrance of honeysuckle abounded through her open window and reminded her of pink and yellow vines growing at her parent's farm. A gentle wind brushed through her honey blonde hair, sweeping it away from her face and shoulders. Groups of Black Angus stood around bales of hay, undisturbed by a young man on horseback galloping through smooth parts of the pastureland. Herds of sheep and goats grazed on grass and other herbage. Shelby passed through a more desolate area and glanced at crumbling homes and tired leaning barns drunken with age, abandoned by early settlers. Wooden structures with original hitching posts, reminiscent of ancestry, appeared infrequently. A group of well-kept homes on carefully preserved farms came into view, and newly constructed buildings where adult children chose to build on their parent's property were obvious. An impressive two-story frame house beside a large white barn at a dairy farm caught her eye. The beginning of sunset cast red and orange hues upon the roof of a building at a ranch next door to a lumber yard and highlighted a luminous shadow of color.

Flowering blooms of summer charmed surroundings that delighted Shelby in simple ways. In a short time, she began to dedicate to the captivating, coal-mining town where local farmers existed from profits of their crops of soybeans, potatoes, wheat, and corn.

Shelby drove further away from town, along a two-lane gravel road, after five miles of more reliable pavement. She smiled and waved toward farmers who gathered their herds and directed their cows toward barns for evening milking, measuring the time of day, and reminding her to turn around at the next opportunity. However, the narrow road restricted such a turn by a border of deep muddy trenches not yet settled by downpours from the previous day. Lengthening shadows began to form a cloudy blanket of gray over the fields. A sudden stillness in the air and absence of activity created a sense of urgency for her to change direction before darkness. Shelby traveled further down the gravel road, hoping to find a lane or a drive upon which to turn around. After passing a thicket of small trees and underbrush, her eye caught a partially concealed bridge made of sturdy planks of wood reaching over a deep trench and leading to an open field. Instinctively, she firmly pressed the brakes of her truck and began to back up, seeking a comprehensive range of roadway. The vehicle turned toward the bridge, but the right front wheel edged into a deep hollow hole spinning with gravel. Shelby's body braced instinctively for impact. Her hands held tightly to the steering wheel as the truck swerved in the direction of a large walnut tree. She gripped the steering wheel, geared up, over-corrected, and lost control. Her truck wavered sideways. She struggled with the steering wheel, but the vehicle jerked with a sweeping blow, slid past the large woody tree trunk, and groaned before settling into a baptismal of sullen silence. The truck tightly wedged between the tree and the bank of the swampy ditch and lacked the power to move when forced. The wheels rotated ineffectively without traction. Her vehicle rocked back and forth like a tired granny in an old rocking chair and lodged deeper into a clump of oozing mud and slough. Shelby stared blankly out the window, wonderstruck. She despaired with hopelessness when she remembered her cell phone on the desk at the newspaper office.

"WHAT WAS I THINKING?" she shouted, "Obviously I wasn't. I don't even have a flashlight." Her spirits sank along with her imprisoned vehicle, which had fallen into a grave of silence. Fixedly staring at a leafy branch spreading wings of drooping leaves onto the mud-splattered windshield, Shelby sought to collect her thoughts. She studied her watch, glassy-eyed, and realized she had sat thirty minutes, imprisoned in her truck.

"I can stay here until morning or make my way up toward the road and take a chance someone will come along," she said aloud, and then assumed her chance of being rescued on the road was decidedly a better idea.

Five

Determined, Shelby took hold of the door handle on the driver's side, but the door wouldn't budge. The decision to leave her vehicle may not be hers. The truck rolled in the muddy trench like a sinking boulder. She crawled across the seat, and with all the strength she could muster, pushed on the passenger door, Her movement caused the truck to roll to the left and fall short of flattening on its side. She froze, afraid to move an inch, but determined not to panic and considered another option after realizing the impossibility of pushing the door upward. Exiting through the back window would require a way to shatter it. The driver's side door was half in the mud and there was a danger of getting pinned underneath if the vehicle shifted further. Her best solution was to climb through the passenger side window if she could climb up. After placing her keys in a small wallet attached with a strap, she slipped the wallet on her wrist, and mentally and physically struggled with great effort to manually roll the window down. Carefully, without causing more sliding movement to the truck, Shelby gripped the frame, and with exhausting effort, pulled her body upward and eased through the small opening of the side window above the door. Once she cleared the window, she collapsed onto the door holding the handle before gliding smoothly down off the passenger door until her bare feet touched a weedy pool of wet sedge and mud. Holding her shoes with one hand and steadying by holding onto her mud-spattered truck with the other hand, Shelby waded through mulls of filth and discarded litter. Her flesh crawled at the thought of stepping on creepy substances. Once on the road, she anxiously searched for a person in the fields, a passing car, truck, tractor, anyone. Shelby was in desperate circumstances and prayed for a miracle.

"NOT EVEN A COW OR HORSE," she shouted, her confidence deflated.

Her instincts, having been brought up in a rural area, told her the local farmers likely finished their chores and had gone home for the day. She remembered the absence of any residential dwellings within the past several miles and despairingly babbled her anguish, "I have driven too far to turn back from where I started. Surely I'll see a farmhouse ahead or a farmer taking his tractor to the barn."

Shelby stepped into her shoes and trudged along the dreaded, narrow road. Soon, a forceful wind and slight mist created a chilled greeting from Mother Nature. The temperature consistently dropped to an unseasonably cool. She braced against the wind, hunched over with her arms huddled against her body, and struggled along, tripping over large rocks.

Thankfully, the wind soon eased briefly, causing an eerie calm, and quieting the trees, enabling her to brisk up her pace. She doggedly moved at a steady pace, keenly observant of any possible means of rescue, but with no one around and no farm or home within sight, she groped her way into nightfall and persistently begged for a miracle. She persistently trudged along and repeatedly stumbled over the graveled road, grinding the thin soles of her flat leather shoes down to the rind of an orange. She suffered bruising and pain to her feet but pushed forward with great effort. Shrilling cries echoed throughout the forest under clouds of gloom.

Suddenly, without warning, a deer exploded through the darkness and bolted directly in front of her. Her body jolted forward as if struck by a blazing flash of lightning.

Shelby lost her balance and tumbled onto the ground before the animal swiftly darted away. She had sensed the warmth from the deer's body by its closeness. Simultaneously, the scream of a hawk vibrated through the trees. A pall of terror cloaked Shelby's body like a hovering tyrant. Her situation had become oppressive, and for long moments she grasped onto a handful of rocks as a child holding on to her mother's skirt, too frightened to move. Gathering her wits, she sucked in a deep breath and exhaled slowly, apprehensive of another terrifying encounter with a wild animal. She grudgingly pulled up from a rocky surface interspersed with wet, spongy moss, and decisively stood, bristling stiff, and gazed at the heavens and Nebulous clouds that overshadowed the indistinct outline of the moon and stars. Rain, accompanied by a sudden violent wind, steadily dribbled upon her head, and streamed down her face. The temperature continued to drop.

Shelby's frustration escalated, "I am soaked and getting miserably colder," she lamented to the darkness. "If a building or house were close by, I wouldn't know without being able to see." She moaned with words barely audible.

She moved forward, teetered back and forth, and stumbled along the dark road for what seemed an eternity.

"Whatever is in store for me? Surely, I will find a farmer going to the fields at daybreak, if I'm still out here, and if I don't get eaten by wild animals," her voice, a voice only she could hear, mocked derisively in an earnest attempt to regain composure with an output of strained humor.

Shelby prayed for her guardian angel to appear, when suddenly, as if her prayer had been answered without hesitancy, approaching lights from half a mile away bounced upon the road. Her expectation of being rescued escalated. The vehicle moved closer. A blanket of sparkling lights swept wings of illumination over shadowy fields and the lonely road.

"Thank God someone's coming," she yelled and charged down the middle of the road. "My nightmare is over."

As the vehicle came closer, fiery headlights beamed rays of brightness over her and virtually penetrated her tan skirt, her thighs telling, revealed above her shapely bare legs. Rain permeated her lustrous pale green blouse and embraced her breast. Her cotton skirt hugged her skin relentlessly with the illusion of wearing nothing underneath. Both her arms waved with ultimate excitement. To her relief, Shelby was going home. A Godsend, an answer to her prayers. Her dilemma had ended.

"STOP!" she shouted. Her body trembled. Her teeth chattered, and in a desperate, demanding plea for help, she yelled again, "STOP! STOP!"

A rickety, tumbledown garbage truck, still equipped with a hopper, and a faded name on the front, POA SANITATION, screeched to an abrupt halt directly in front of her. Shelby held firm in the middle of the narrow gravel road. But, at once, two loud and drunken or drugged hoodlums dressed in army fatigues pounced out both open doors. They stumbled heavily toward her, and with shrilly piercing voices, yelled obnoxious obscenities. A chilling and painful shock entered her body. Her hopes of being rescued abruptly vanished as a vaporous mist. The smell of danger engulfed her.

"Look what we done got here, an angel landed down right in front of us," one of them drooled while the other one barked strong suggestive language.

Shelby shrieked in horror as they awkwardly lunged toward her sounding off whistles and eerie laughter. She trembled into a level of defenselessness, bolted away from the headlights, and frantically searched for an escape route. Her heart was pulsed in high frequency and her body moved with astounding agility over a pile of rocks toward the edge of forest. Her feet suffered in agony upon jagged rocks. The larger man, the size of a small bear, lost his balance as he thrust his arms and extended his reach to seize his prize. Suddenly, the other one, the one with an unruly dark beard, tripped and awkwardly stepped into a pile of cow manure alongside the road. He yelled heinous obscenities at her.

"Now see here what you done made me do!" he shouted, inflamed with violence. "Donnie, go git her, she's gitten away."

"Come here, girlie, we ain't gonna hurt you," the other one guilefully pleaded.

The men howled mournfully in pursuit of their intended pleasure. They tripped across the road in a drunken stupor, grabbed at her, and clumsily slammed into each other like two drunken gunslingers tossed out swinging doors of an old Western saloon.

A frightening sense of urgency overcame her. Shelby scrambled as a wild animal running from a burning forest. She leaped across more piles of gravel toward a wire fence, frantic to escape. Vowing not to give in to defeat, and without glancing over her shoulder, She dove headfirst over a low section of bent metal fencing. She scraped her arms and legs on rusted barbed wire and sank like a rag doll into a dark wetted down marsh. After recovering from the fall, Shelby sullenly bent close to the ground and used her hands to grope and scratch blindly through the brush. She crawled on her knees through dense masses of a thicket of weeds and further into darkness in a formidable effort to escape. Her legs quivered like bowls of gelatin while struggling through a field of tangled weeds. She fought through a clump of wet, prickly plants that inflicted her with sharp tingling pain and clambered to free herself.

"Will they come after me?" Shelby brokenly gasped and strived to move faster. Distance came slowly with nature's obstacles hindering her progress. Ignoring punishment to her face and body, she pummeled through the thick woodland. After crawling over wooded obstacles, a rush of energy compelled her body to stand and move quickly. She bounced over clumps of high weeds, broken branches, and fallen trees, struggling to put as much distance as possible between her and the two dangerous thugs. Shelby pulled and twisted her arms and legs through gangling wet weeds until falling over a large decaying branch.

The two crazed ruffians positioned their truck horizontally across the road to illuminate the fields to find her. When the vegetation surrounding her fiercely glared from the haunting lights, she trembled with fear and remained still with her face pressed into wet soil and half-buried leaves. Terrified, she listened to the truck as it sat idling, thrashing like an old washing machine on its last leg.

When overcome by their failure to carry off their intended prey, the two drunks repeated a pattern of pacing awkwardly back and forth in front of their battered truck as spent sailors on leave. Without warning, a sudden blast of wind and a stinging shower of rain prompted them to climb loathingly into their resounding vehicle. Lights from the dilapidated garbage truck dimmed. The motor stopped. The men attempted to lure the young woman out of the woods by deceiving her into believing they had left. Shelby stayed covertly hidden. Minutes seemed like hours to her until the motor on the garbage truck revved again. The desperadoes spitefully gave in. They engaged in relentless fury by their defeat and clamorously bellowed obscenities into the darkness at their intended victim and at each other for allowing her to escape. The old truck vibrated and violently rattled along the road with music blaring until its taillights faded through a fog of darkness and misty rain. The truck had vanished. Dreaded formidable harm, at least by humans, ended, a relief to Shelby, who, commanded by fear, lay motionless for more long minutes. When convinced her assailants had gone, she stood upright, trembled with fear, and stared blankly into the darkness. Drops of rain swept upon leafy vegetation. She instinctively spat grass and wiped away weeds from her bleeding face, arms, and legs. Her wet and muddy clothing glued fast to her frame. Her flat-soled shoes, damaged beyond repair, squished with water but were essential for her to move.

Six

"What now? Where to go from here?" Shelby muttered, somewhat calmed by the sound of her own voice. Barely breathing those questions while sucking night air into her lungs, she began to process what she previously endured and then, continued to limp wearily through the wild. She shivered from fear and the elements and defensively moved through dense wet weeds populated by mosquitoes and other unidentifiable critters. Determined to remain out of sight and away from the driving lane, Shelby, forcefully, propelled for hours through gangling walls of overgrown vegetation. Screams and shrieking cries of animals pierced the wilderness and fiercely haunted the night, terrifying her. She was an alien in animal dominated woods.

Lethargic and languished by fatigue, she sluggishly maneuvered her body toward a thicket of weeping willow trees where she slid slowly against a tree trunk and collapsed in a depleted slump under the obscurity of thick extending branches.

"What will become of me?" Shelby sobbed to the heavens. She cringed at repeating sounds of dread which had seized the night and dominated her thoughts. Exhaustion from extreme physical and mental fatigue overcame her. She huddled against the tree, concealed behind drooping wet leaves, and shifted her mind to her parents, her former co-workers, and Tony, the boyfriend she left when it became clear he aspired a more lasting relationship. One she did not share. She gladdened her accomplishments and feared for her goals not yet reached.

Paralyzed by fear and the vaunting haunts of nature, she expelled air from her lungs through whimpering defeat, closed her eyes to avoid eyes staring back, and partially sheltered from drizzling rain, soon fell fast asleep under a hazy moon.

She had no perception of the real-life chilling drama about to dispossess her vision of a brand-new beginning or of secrets held by a few who destined to change her life forever.

As hints of dawn approached, Shelby stood, cautiously turned about, barely able to see the ground under her, and reverently faced the tree under which she slept. She prayed a prayer of thankfulness, blessing the tree for comforting and sheltering her. She had recalled a book where she had read, "The willow tree represents strength, hope, and safety". She gazed incredulously at the vast, untamed forest still faded by clouds of darkness, alone as a lonely wildflower in a field of untamed wilderness. Shelby praised God for protecting her during the night and gathering the hem of her skirt began to blot plastered mud and fragments of debris from her face and scratched skin.

"WHERE ARE THE CROPS?" She yelled and scanned the area in bewilderment. "No farmhouses, barns, cattle, or fields of corn and wheat yet visible, only weeds and wild animals."

The deprivation of food and water under sheer exhaustion contributed to her weakened condition. She had lost power of perceiving the direction of the road and looked for guidance of the moon to avoid going back the way she had come. Dense patches of gangling weeds and thorn bushes poked up through the ground like sharp needles reminding her to tread carefully. The fear of contracting poison vines hidden along the underbrush was insignificant compared to facing dreaded treacherous snakes and wild beasts. Shelby dragged her body through strenuous exertion in anticipation of coming upon a house or someone out early working in the fields. Her eyes searched for crops, a light from a home or a barn, and for someone in a pasture.

Seven

Shelby had no clue as to where the road was from her vantage point. Impulsively, she stopped, shrank to her knees, and raised her arms upward toward the sky and prayed for guidance.

Instantly, the earth beneath her feet gently rumbled, suggesting waving motions of an earthquake about to happen. Startled, she shuddered and wavered unsteadily. When a twisted bundle of hay brushed lightly by her face and floated upward toward the sky, she looked up and stared in awe at the most profound beauty she had ever seen. A brilliance of green and blue plumes of spectacular color reached beneath a mass of fleecy white clouds, washed over the fields, and hypnotized her into fearless attention. A patch of fresh air conspicuously swirled about her face. Her hair softly brushed across her eyes and blew upward as if she were falling gracefully from the heavens, but she was unable to move. It appeared the earth was standing still. An eerie silence swept the area. There was no chirping of birds, no rain, no wind, or sounds coming from the wild. She stood, bristling stiff, upon a grassy surface interspersed with spongy moss and could barely feel her feet touching the ground. She gazed at the heavens and breathed in a sweet fragrance of fresh-cut flowers and pine needles. An overpowering peace descended over her and throughout her body. Something soft brushed her face; an amorphous of no shape or pattern fluttered in front of her face urging her to change directions. Beaconed by the apparition, she compelled to obey and instinctively did an about-turn. When she did so, the magnificent radiance grew in blinding intensity as if praising the heavens, and in a sudden bolt of electricity, shot upward through a pearly sky into darkness. And then, without warning, just as suddenly, the atmosphere awakened as if turned on by a switch. Birds began to sing, and soft rustling of leaves upon the ground started to scatter.

"Is this a mirage luring me toward something nonexistent?" she questioned aloud. "Am I delusional? Did what I thought I experienced really happen?"

Shelby focused on the flash of lights and mysterious brush against her cheek, and slowly began to move in the direction prompted by the image. A few moments passed, and then, a miraculously beautiful scene appeared on the horizon. She strolled numbly forward.

"Is this an illusion?" She blinked her eyes and shook her head from side to side to determine what was real and not a fraction of light rays creating a mirage. She blinked again. Her eyes fell upon a lake surrounded by a thicket of small trees. A horse grazing upon a green carpet of meadow stood several feet away from her. She stared for several minutes at the semblance of an enchanting oasis and began to move quickly through the field. She watched the horse gracefully gallop away. Her heart raced, increasing her energy and resistance to fatigue. Her forbidding grimness faded, confident God's angels had reached out and touched her. She urged her body to endure, and with renewed strength, made her way into the vast field.

Easing closer to the lake, Shelby flattened upon the ground and scooped clear water into her mouth and over her face. She dazedly lingered, unable to think clearly and staggered across the grass to sit upon on a large fallen tree trunk. She sat for a long while and gazed at the picturesque landscape of breathtaking beauty; the lake, and sloping hills leading to a valley below. Wildflowers, groups of trees, and clumps of bushes seized her attention. The physical features of the terrain inspired her senses as an artist. She gazed out as far as she could see through the morning haze at the meadow. The tranquil morning air, the lake encircled by evergreens, and the land, entranced her very soul. It was a sharp contrast compared to the tangled forest through which she struggled.

"This is the kind of place people write songs about," Shelby said aloud. After resting, she collected her senses, and with impelling force, urged her body to move forward in the direction from where she had seen the horse gallop. When unable to push her body further, she sat upon the grassy meadow to rest. Suddenly, she noticed a faint, steady illumination glaring in the distance. Slowly, she stumbled to her feet and continued along her chosen path, soon to see the light flicker through the trees. The shadow of a building emerged. Shelby determined, it was possibly a lantern glowing from outside a barn or house. The light shone brighter as she approached.

She had lost the power of feeling in her arms and legs and was forced to rest upon the ground. She rubbed her legs for more circulation, after which she put her hands over her eyes, and considered what might lay in the path ahead. A grayish cloud of fog stilled the area.

"I can't take any chances," she fretfully whispered. "The possibility the two drunks might reappear is frightening. "But My choices are few," she mumbled, glaring at the lantern. "No one knows where I am, and my truck may sit undiscovered for days. Likely, no one will miss me until Monday."

Shelby took possession of her senses and chose to trust the empyrean suggestion that descended from the heavens. She seized strength enough to lift herself up and over a wire fence where she cautiously moved in a stooped position across an orchard of fruit trees. She overcame the voice inside her whispering fear of another desperate encounter and crossed a field of open land toward another patch of a grassy meadow. A black, planked, wooden fence, used to keep livestock inside, appeared before her. She skillfully maneuvered through two slightly separated planks and onto a patch of shorter grass, not knowing what lay ahead. Lingering fog obscured a broader view of the area. Shelby's inescapable reasoning to continue the chosen course outweighed the alternative, which was to return to the wild.

Cautions roared at her, persuading her to kneel and crouch behind a thick row of border hedges. Seconds later, she moved stealthily, in a bent position, and crept onto a lawn carpeted with neatly cut, folded blades of green grass. She inched toward the light, attentive to her surroundings, crouched with her knees bent, and shifted closer toward the entrance of an enormous barn. She slowly edged toward a hinged door and willed her body sideways to wriggle through the door without pushing it further. Tuneful vibrations filled the air with indiscernible sounds of breathing inside the barn. Shelby crept along a wall fitted with independent stalls and peered, with glazed vision, over the tops of two-part doors. She glared into the eyes of animals separated by species. A few lazily glowered at her making lowing sounds of lazy doldrums.

"Two appear much as a bear with its cub," she cringed.

Shelby hesitated at the barn entrance and waited until dark clouds softly drifted upward. She then hid behind shrubs next to a fence and waited for daylight to begin to fall upon the earth, exposing more of her surroundings. Once, more land came into view, her eyes focused on another barn, a horse stable, and a compound of buildings in the distance. Her attention averted to her immediate left where she saw a thicket of shrubs and tall trees, and the faint silhouette of a large house mimicking a reproduction from a Margaret Mitchell novel.

"Wow!" she whispered. "Have I fallen through a hole like Alice, and into a beautiful make-believe underground world?

She stood, mesmerized by the surroundings. A nearby lily pond and a lush garden filled with flowering plants caught her eye.

"Impressive, this farm reminds me of historic horse farms in Lexington,

Kentucky. Extraordinarily fine!" she whispered.

Shelby's eyes filled with amazement at such a home compared to dwellings she passed when driving through the countryside. She paused, stirred by a bit of magic and wonderment of such an extravagant house, and surrounding properties beautified by nature.

"This is so beyond typical for this area," she said aloud.

Upon moving closer to tall trees surrounding the three-story brick house, her imagination captured its aesthetic appeal. Shelby gazed in awe at the stately residence, enhanced by slender upright pillars. The house, she assumed, was worthy of the noble, much as a governor's grand residence.

"Have I stepped into a movie set?" she said aloud. "This is extraordinary, a mansion at the very least.

Shelby lingered quietly, shivered from the elements and fear of the unknown and stared at the house for several minutes. She scanned the surrounding area and edged her way toward a side entrance. Her hands trembled like a bowl of fast simmering broth when she awkwardly reached out and timidly knocked on a grand white door. After what seemed a reasonable time for someone to respond, the house hushed in silence. Another knock on the door and still no activity, not a voice or even the bark of a dog. Shelby breathed in profoundly and aggressively reached for the door for the third time. She lost her balance, causing her foot to slam against the casing. The door easily glided open. She tumbled unsteadily over the threshold and banged her head on the floor of a large sitting room. Dazed by the fall, Shelby lay flat for long seconds, lost in a dreamy blur.

With careful regard and wobbling with wavering mobility, she clambered upright. Fear mingled with reverence as she froze before a magnificently bizarre collection of architectural design, flavored in decor themes. She crept to the center of the room, drawn to a stone fireplace with a glowing log among burnt embers. Shelby stood by the fire and gratefully warmed her chilled body.

"Hello, is anyone home?" she called. Still no answer.

In desperation, she yelled, "HELLO, IS ANYONE HERE?" Shelby's voice rippled through painful sounds of stress, affected by the horror she had encountered, and elements she had faced during the night.

"This is a museum," she sighed. "Outstanding paintings, elaborate wall decor, and exquisitely colorful quilts elegantly placed on a rack are only the most pedestrian of the contents," she spoke idly, gazing about the room. "The floor of this magnificent room glows with shiny bricks and hardened clay depicting a relaxed country atmosphere. Everything reveals a great eye for detail and a designers' taste."

Shelby remained by the fire and quietly gazed at the textured ceiling, captivated by the elegance of such a country home. Suddenly, she jumped, startled at a man's voice from the doorway.

"The room is intense, isn't it?"

Eight

Christopher Stone grew up knowing he was adopted. Born in Florence, Italy, he traveled the world with his adoptive parents until he became of school-age, and the family settled in California, the Stone's home State. Christopher completed his studies in the United States, gained citizenship, and became attached to the country in which he became a part. Through efforts of his adoptive parents, he came face-to-face with his birth mother, Maria, at the age of twenty-one. Mother and son soon developed an endearing relationship. They wrote back and forth to each other frequently and, on occasion, visited.

After Christopher graduated from law school, tragedy struck. His parents, the Stones, succumbed to a fiery plane crash over Egypt, which caused a tremendous void in Stone's life. He and Maria grieved together over the loss of his adoptive parents, and the two of them formed a natural bond as mother and son. They moved together into a rented apartment close to Hollywood, where Stone engaged with the American motion-picture industry. At his request, Stone's his mother, Maria Villella, a retired Russian ballet dancer, began talking to her son about his father, who had met with a tragic drowning before Christopher's birth. Maria believed Giovanni Sforza, Chris's father, was murdered. She described his death as an intentional murderous plot covered up by members of the Carabinieri, and not an accidental drowning as officially recorded.

Grieving over the loss of her lover and believing she must give up her son for him to live a better life, a life with two parents to love him as much as she, Maria had allowed the adoption. To enter her son's life in later years brought more happiness to Maria than she ever imagined.

Stone's career advanced quickly. Significantly because of his integrity and boundless energy. He had become interested in the film industry because of one of his professors, an accomplished actor who constantly talked about his experiences in class. Stone's reputation as a filmmaker/director soon gained eminence among distinguished names in the industry of filmmaking. Honored in his late twenties with notable success and international acclaim, Christopher Stone's peers dubbed him as one of the distinct breeds of filmmakers of a younger generation. As his career advanced along with a substantial income, Christopher doted on his Mother. He showered her with gifts and affection. He proudly introduced her to prestigious events concerning his business. She delighted in watching him grow in his profession as a celebrated artist and as a respected member of the community.

At the beginning of his career, Stone had befriended a young actress who asked his advice in raising her young son. Lana Carlina had ended a failing marriage and viewed Stone as a role model for her child. She asked Stone to mentor young Jason, not wanting the boy to follow his father's destructive ways or mimic either parent by becoming an actor. Stone became attached to the boy and volunteered to care for him in her absence. At one point, seeing the frustration the boy suffered by living with a mother who busied herself with a career, an alternative was offered. Instead of leaving the boy under the supervision of an unimpressionable nanny and moving him from one location to another, young Jason moved primarily to the Stone home, closer to his school. The move was regarded in favor by the boy's mother, Stone's mom, Maria, and Ms. Maude, Stone's faithful housekeeper. Those, in the Stone home, persuaded a positive influence on the boy through his formidable years, treating him as a family member. However, once he graduated from college, Jason became an accomplished actor.

"Stone facetiously explained to the boy's mother, "Must be in the genes."

Stone spoiled his mother with determination against her protests. On her fiftieth birthday, he escorted her to a car dealership where he insisted, Maria select the sports car of her dreams, sparing no expense. Finally, he persuaded her to decide. Her choice was a red Lamborghini Diablo of Italy. He arranged to have the vehicle delivered to give her a chance to get used to driving such a unique, sophisticated car in a safer and less congested area.

For another celebration, Stone, now in his late twenties, approached his mother with a plan to investigate his father's death. Christopher supported his mother, who believed his father's death was not the result of an accident. Circumstantial details characterizing Maria's suspicions and suspicions of others of how Sforza died led to the decision to go to Italy. Maria had told her son how family and friends of Sforza's believed a conspiracy of silence concealed the circumstances of his father's untimely death. She believed Italian police were involved in the crime.

Stone vowed one day he would seek the truth. After becoming a well-established Hollywood movie producer possessing resources to investigate and to search for answers to his father's drowning, the search became a reality. Maria embraced the idea, and immediately, Stone planned a trip for the two of them to travel to Italy, where they hoped to uncover evidence to reopen the case of Giovanni Sforza's death.

The two of them, Stone, and his mother, excited with the plan, set out to celebrate their decision over dinner.

Maria navigated her sleek sports car through the winding hills of Los Angeles with Chris alongside in the passenger seat. She was a safe driver and familiar with the treacherous bending curves on a path leading from Chris's newly purchased estate. Their home was nestled high in the hills of Los Angeles, where neighbors lived on gaited properties and where everyone had at least one expensive sports vehicle in their garage. However, speeding had become a nuisance, especially by young people. Maria learned, early on, to observe others with extreme caution.

Maria drove the same route the two had driven before, practicing, and familiarizing with her new car. The weather was clear and pleasant enough for an open-top. Maria's long golden hair blew wildly in the wind as she drove down a steep hill. The two talked about their up-and-coming trip to Italy and the anticipation of meeting with Chris's paternal relatives.

Maria laughed at some of Chris's childhood escapades he shared with her. He told her how he had been adventurous and challenged himself against what his parents accepted on specific issues, and how his parents explained the consequences if he repeated hair-raising events. He said, often after they scolded him, he walked away, listening to the two of them chuckle at his cleverness. They loved him dearly, and he, them. Maria was grateful to the Stones and told her son how they had kept her abreast of all his schoolwork. She knew he was happy by his expression in the photos they sent to her of each of his accomplishments and birthday celebrations. She told him, for the first time, she had attended his school events, including his high-school and college graduations, and how she stayed in the background out of respect for the Stones. He smiled at his mother with all the love in his heart. She turned toward him and smiled back. That's when the accident occurred.

Maria drove up a steep hill around a curve when a driver in a pick-up approached downward too fast from the opposite direction. The driver overcorrected to avoid going over an embankment and ran his pick-up over easement gravel. His vehicle blew out a tire and plunged across the road, slamming violently into the Lamborghini. Chris remained hospitalized for two weeks with lacerations and a broken pelvis. The mental anguish and suffering for having lost his mother, once again, inflicted a burden of mental torment far exceeding his physical pain. Maria and the driver of the truck died at the scene.

Nine

Weighted with guilt for surviving the accident in which his mother perished, Christopher Stone opted for a silent refuge to meditate and escape disciplined routines and what he referred to as the scrambles of Hollywood. He claimed to his peers and the press he had taken an extended holiday, a sabbatical of sorts.

"For a year, maybe two," he told them.

He postponed the search into his father's death he had planned with his beloved mother and traveled incognito to avoid crowds and to escape recognition.

In a remote county in Kentucky, Stone became Christopher Standish and moved into a rented home with his faithful servant, Ms. Maude Hopkins. Ms. Maude had remained at his side throughout his recovery, mothering him through his low spirits of depression. Only a select few of his peers were privy to his where-a-bouts.

After six months of living somewhat in isolation, Standish became intrigued by the county in which he lived and began to delve into political and economic issues of the county and the State of Kentucky. He became acquainted with members of the town council and volunteered his services to the community and donated to the school system. Standish enjoyed the undisturbed quiet of the country and bought several acres of land on where a home surrounded by a landscape bathed with nature's magnificence came to life. The enhanced beauty of the setting flourished with new trees, flowers, a glacial blue swimming pool, and a luxury pool house. Newly constructed barns and private dwellings suitable for farmhands and their families were developed at a distance much like a small community. A private playground and park, compliments of Mr. Stanford, offered recreation for the children of the workers.

Chris intended to utilize the farm as a vacation spot, a retreat for himself and his peers, but his time at the farm became increasingly important. In time, he planned to divide his time between his business in California and the farm. He became more dedicated to the farm, and included harboring and affectionately tending to previously abused animals, saving several destined for destruction. Christopher Standish lived a peaceful life. He became known to residents in the area and had developed friendships with neighbors who referred to him fondly as Noah. Locals came to view Standish as an entrepreneur, a wealthy gentleman farmer. People respected him and his dedication to the county and his political views. He utilized some of his assets to help establish a small hospital in town. Soon, his interest in the governmental growth of the county escalated. His interest in managing political affairs along with members of the school board escalated and he became a member of the city council. Standish sold his estate in Hollywood, intending to buy a smaller place in which to stay when commuting to California. Kentucky had become his primary residence.

Standish's rural neighbors knew little about his personal life, other than what they observed, his government interests, and his frequent travel.

Stone, alias Standish, still in his mid-thirties, lived much as a hermit until Jason visited. Jason had completed filming a movie and readied to extend his stay at the farm until he determined a course toward a goal or possibly an alternate profession.

Standish and Jason enjoyed working together and alongside the farmhands taking care of the land and animals.

Jason loved the farm and learned to ride horses and drive a tractor. Stone, as a surrogate parent, had gained affection for the youngster when Jason lived at Stone's residence in Hollywood. Stone had supported him in tryouts in sports and school plays as a parent or older brother would have. He urged him to study hard in school and attend college. He guided him toward success by encouraging him to have confidence in his ability to weigh his options clearly and to have the courage of his convictions. The two became like father and son, and later, because of closeness in age, as brothers. As Jason matured, the two men talked over business matters and politics, trusting, and supporting one another. Jason became a respected, talented actor, and like Stone, he desired to achieve more in life than fame and fortune. Chris had detected restlessness in his young friend and encouraged him to stay at the Standish farm until he worked through his goals and ambitions.

After a time at the farm, Jason encouraged Chris to resume his plan to visit Italy and locate relatives of his father and pursue the truth behind his father's death.

"It's what Maria would want," Jason told him.

"Is this what they refer to as a role reversal?" Chris asked.

Jason shrugged his shoulders, flashed his familiar boyish grin, and left for the barn to tend the animals.

Chris mulled over Jason's words of wisdom for a few days before he conceded.

"You are right, Maria would applaud the decision," He told Jason. "I am going to plan a trip to visit Italy.

Ten

Chris arrived in Florence in May during the off-season without the clamor of multitudes of tourists crowding the streets. The average daily temperature ranged in the '70s and '80s. After he settled in a suite at JK Place Firenze, a former residence in Piazza Santa Maria Novella in central Florence, Chris hired a driver. He visited the Laurentian Library, where, with the help of an interpreter, he found families with the last name, Sforza. His search led to the obituary of Benito Sforza, the brother of Giovanni, and then to Benito's two surviving sons, Lorenzo, and Josef Sforza, both businessmen and owners of a woolen textile factory. Chris placed a call to the factory and talked to either of the Sforza brothers. Joseph had taken the call and skeptical to hear from someone surfacing as their lost relative after thirty years. The brothers distrusted a sudden claim of kinship by the stranger. However, the men agreed to meet in the evening at a small café in the public square called Piazza della Signoria, a tourist attraction and gathering spot for locals.

Before meeting the brothers, Chris toured the city of his birth for the first time as an adult. The visit was his first opportunity to study the country and the culture of its people. Deciding to learn the language and culture of his heritage, he visited famous art museums, including Uffizi Palace and Galleria dell' Accademia, where he discovered medieval sculptures of masterpieces such as Michelangelo's stone statue of David. He browsed in elegant shopping centers in the western part of an old section of the city and bought a few artifacts and had them shipped to his farm.

That afternoon, when Chris arrived at the café, he realized he had little knowledge of how to identify the brothers, but when he circled the bar and walked past their table looking around the room, the Sforza brothers gasped. They both stood, glared at Chris, and then stared at each other in disbelief. At first glance, the brothers realized Chris's resemblance to their family. They became overwhelmed beyond words when they stared at the man who mirrored how they remembered their uncle Gio. The two brothers, around the same height and weight as Chris, resembled a definite kinship. The three of them might have passed as brothers. They were, indeed, kinsmen.

After a brief introduction and credibility confirmed, an immediate celebration began with Lorenzo shouting the introduction of his long lost cousin. He ordered the finest wine available, and nearly everyone nearby joined in the celebration with salutes and cheers. Josef ordered wine for other tables. A homecoming praiseworthy of remembrance developed. As in any reunion, events began to surface through family photographs, updates, and history.

The brothers remembered their Uncle Giovanni with admiration. They shared stories and told Chris of his father's reputation as an expert fisherman and skilled swimmer. Josef described how their grandfather was animatedly convinced Giovanni's death was a murderous plot to keep him separated from Maria. The family denied all claims of Gio having perished by accident.

"Three decades have passed since Uncle Gio's lifeless body emerged from waters of the Mediterranean Sea," Lorenzo said. "Our family still grieves. He was our hero."

"He taught us how to fish and swim and played ball with us as we grew from small children," said Josef.

The Sforza brothers were young children at the time but remembered Maria as pretty and kind.

"She often brought gifts to the family and played games with us as children," said

Lorenzo.

Chris explained how Maria had planned to accompany him on his visit to Italy before the fateful accident.

"We are so sorry," said Josef, and he and his brother motioned the sign of the cross and said a prayer.

"Our family failed to find proof of wrongdoing, but we remained dedicated to the search for the truth until our father, Benito, died at the age of sixty from a heart attack. We believe evidence covered up by officials would prove our uncle was a victim of foul play. Our papa and grandpapa convinced the family that an assassin was paid for by either Maria's family or someone connected to the Russian ballet company where she performed."

"Uncle Gio's death devastated our family," said Josef, "After Grandpapa died, our Papa talked to people about Maria. He found she had given birth to a son, but secrecy formed around the names of your adopted parents. Papa pressed for information, but officials claimed to have sealed contents describing the whereabouts of Maria or the child. Another tragedy for our family.

"Maria never revisited us. We understood either her family took charge or people from the Ballet Company enticed her to return to the Ballet. Our parents said she left vulnerable, and with a broken heart."

"Are there more of my father's relatives in this area?" Chris asked.

"Yes! In addition to our sons and their families, aunt Gina Sforza, our father's younger sister is an artist. She lives in Rome, is in her late fifties, unmarried, and lives alone. She supports herself by painting portraits and landscapes," said Josef.

"I would like very much to see her," Chris told them.

"What a wonderful surprise for our aunt. We will not tell her beforehand of your visit with us," said Lorenzo.

The rest of the visit, after several bottles of wine, centered on Chris's life in America and the lives of his cousins and their families. The next morning the brothers escorted their cousin to visit the gravesite of their uncle Giovanni. Chris stood with his head bowed for several minutes staring at the tombstone of his father. Then he parted with directions on how to locate his aunt Gina, and enough information to warrant a closer examination into his father's mysterious drowning.

Eleven

The crisp morning air swept a welcoming calm throughout the atmosphere when Chris reached central Italy and to the Capital city of Rome. A hired driver drove him through a sun sparked dewy landscape before delivering him to a quaint pension in the center of town. His cousins had recommended the up-scale boarding-house primarily because management catered to prominent businesspeople.

Once settled, Chris walked to the forum and alongside markets and public office buildings, mingling among pedestrians from all walks of life. He regarded ancient architectural structures, including St. Peters Basilica on the site of the old St. Peter's church. He marveled at works of art and witnessed the spiritual energy one gets from Michelangelo's paintings. At the library, he spent time reading the history of The West Roman and The Byzantine Empires. He continued to explore the area for a while, returned to the pension, ate lunch, and summoned his driver, Pierre. Pierre was French but spoke perfect Italian and English. The two set out to locate the address his cousins had given him.

They drove by apartment buildings cramped beside one another, through hills, along fields of golden sunflowers, and spreading acres dotted with vibrant wildflowers until reaching flat land. They passed rural villages and simple adobe dwellings. They drove in-depth into the countryside along the glistening Tiber River, where Chris glanced at different colorful houses built by wealthy landowners. Some of the houses, structured around atriums, were windowless with roof openings for light and air.

After another thirty minutes of driving, Pierre drove down a narrow cobblestone street where a group of fifteenth-century luxury villas stood adjacent to a park. Flowering window boxes adorned the villas, adding color and sweet fragrance to the ambient air. The car slowed and gently came to a stop where Chris exited and walked toward a villa shielded by a marble stone wall behind a boundary of thick green hedges. A variety of flowers painted a brilliant fence along the path to the entrance of the address he held in his hand.

Chris paused outside the car. He surveyed the area when his attention centered upon a woman in the park. The park, sprinkled with geraniums, plumeria, budding trees of bougainvillea, and rose trellises, was adorned with colorful benches. Visitors, often held captive by the ornamental beauty and interest the park bestowed, returned often. The woman sat near a lily pond boarded by roses and other flowering bushes. She continued to concentrate on the work before her, oblivious to her surroundings.

Chris walked toward the woman. He crept slowly behind her, keeping his distance so as not to disturb her concentration. The petite woman, with her face inconspicuously shielded by a floppy hat, sat upon a short stool. With her long skirt and colorful tunic, or painter's smock, she added a blithe spirit to the natural surroundings. With brush in hand, the artist faced an easel supporting a canvas on which she stroked a brush upon the face of a strikingly handsome woman. At first glance, the face on the canvas was familiar to Chris, but he realized the portrait was unfinished. He watched for several seconds, attentive to the controlled movement of the artist's hand as she gently stroked a slender brush across the canvas, creating a delicate streak of pinkish-white above her subject's head.

Chris peacefully approached from behind the woman to where she would have a front view of him. He didn't want to startle her by walking up from behind. However, when Gina Sforza's eyes focused upon the man opposite her, she screamed and jolted her body so abruptly her stool tilted backward. Her hat hurled upon the ground, and her easel toppled over, threatening to damage the painting. For an instant, she believed she was dying and envisioning images of past lives. Startled, Chris jumped quickly and saved the day by bringing the painting and easel to stand upright before it reached the ground.

"I am sorry, I didn't mean to frighten you," he said, calmly handing her hat to her.

She stared at him; her lips quivered for several seconds before she spoke.

"Ms. Sforza?" he asked.

He knew by her sudden reaction, and by the surprising resemblance she shared with her nephews, she was the sister of his father. She was an attractive woman. Younger than he had envisioned. He wondered why she had never married.

"Who are you?" she demanded. Her knees wobbled, and her face, with a beyond belief expression, turned pale. She leveled her arms out to steady herself. She imagined the man before her, the spirit of her deceased brother. The woman held her chest as if she expected to be dying from a heart attack.

Chris, delighted to find her English as precise as his own, quickly established his identity as the son of her brother, Giovanni. Aunt Gina's eyes widened. She backed away, still glaring at him.

She lowered toward her stool, sat down, and stared in disbelief, but unmistaken similarities spoke the truth. Stunned, captured as if in a hypnotic trance, Gina blinked stares at him for seconds as if awakening from a fantasy dream. She stood and reached her arms up to stroke his face as if the illusion would fade. Aunt Gina stared at him, wide-eyed, with her head tilted to one side as if afraid if she closed her eyes, he would disappear. After his Aunt's recovery from shock, and all the tears and Mama Mia's subsided, Chris told her of his visit with her nephews, his cousins. Once she gathered her wits, she thoughtfully invited her nephew into her villa, where they shared sweetened cakes with cheese and fruit. She opened a bottle of her best wine in celebration. After getting better acquainted and bringing each other up to date on family, he told his aunt of his intention to ascertain if his father died in an accident or murdered as suspected.

"YOU ARE SENT BY GOD," she cried out. "God has sent you to us."

She called her nephews in Florence to share her delight of uniting with her nephew and playfully shamed them for keeping such a secret from her for even one minute. Afterward, she brought family photo albums to share with Chris. He stared at his astonishing resemblance to his father.

"This is like looking into a mirror," he told her. "Now I understand your shock when you saw me."

A photograph of Giovanni Sforza posing in all his fishing gear aboard a sizeable commercial boat docked at a busy shore was the first photograph Chris had seen of his father. It brought tears to his eyes. Aunt Gina smiled and hugged her nephew again, grateful to have united with the son of her precious brother. The Sforza family had no inclination Christopher Stone, the famed Hollywood superstar moviemaker with a Spielberg reputation was their lost loved one. The Sforza family enjoyed movies, especially Aunt Gina.

"If only we had paid attention to your celebrity pictures," Aunt Gina said.

Gina asked about his mama, and then she sorrowfully turned from him in prayer for several seconds. Chris stared at a photograph of a strikingly handsome and happy young couple. A glowing Maria, about five or six months pregnant, stood alongside Giovanni, a proud expectant father. Another photo pictured Maria in a graceful pose during the Ballet's rendition of Sleeping Beauty, costumed in white silk tricot, readied for the performance.

"They secretly planned a wedding," Aunt Gina told him.

"I can't understand why Maria failed to tell me about relatives of my father in Italy until much later," Chris said to his aunt.

"Perhaps talking about Gio's family would have awakened sorrowful memories for her," Aunt Gina said, "Maria and Gio were as one. Visiting his family without him might have been unbearable for her.

"Your mama—so exceptional and so beautiful. We all loved her. The portrait I am working on is of her. She is a favorite subject for me to put on canvas. I stored it for years and recently brought it out for completion. How extraordinary you would come along at the exact instant I started work on the painting. It is a spiritual omen, a gift from God. After a few finishing touches, the portrait is yours. I want you to take it with you."

"Please, let me pay you," he offered.

"No! We are family," she said, and then insisted he stay at her villa. The Sforza family had instantly accepted their newly found relative with love and attachment.

"Thank you. I will cherish the painting forever. And yes, I am honored to stay here with you if my visit does not inconvenience you," Chris told his aunt. "I can return with my things tomorrow."

Chris and his Aunt Gina delighted in the joy of having found one another. They talked for another hour: about his mom, the Sforza family, his adoptive family, his business, her paintings, etc. And then Christopher left with his driver, Pierre.

The following day after he returned, he and his Aunt Gina's decided on an investigator to search for information into his father's death. Chris acquired the services of a local private detective, Carlo Guinizelli. Guinizelli would later join Jack Cravens, Chris's detective friend from the States, who would assist in the investigation.

Twelve

"Hello!" *the voice* was unobtrusive, a quiet baritone.

Shelby sprang to attention. She turned to face a gentleman standing in the entry hall. His arms folded across his chest. Dressed in charcoal gray overalls and knee-high black boots, she marveled at his shoulder-length hair, pure white as perfect snow contrasting against his tanned face. Her eyes widened. Shelby realized, as he began to move closer, he was a younger man than he appeared from across the room.

His dark eyebrows lifted, waiting for her to speak.

Shelby hesitated. He took her breath away. He was tall; a tower of dignity and fitness, emphasized by his stately posture. A Venetian nobleman came to her mind at first glance.

After an awkward moment of staring into penetrating, gentle brown eyes, she straightened her body, choked out a breath, and spoke quietly with a soft raspy voice, "Oh! I am sorry." Embarrassed and self-conscious, Shelby blushed a humble apology. She realized she must appear as a savage beast or street urchin.

"Your door opened when I knocked, and I need help," she stammered.

"Well, young lady," he responded calmer than she expected. "How can I help you, my dear?" his curious eyes mirrored a sympathetic audience.

Shelby, conscious of having left dirt in the room, shyly stumbled through an introduction. Tears streaked down her swollen, bloody face as she recounted her drive into the country and her desperate escape from an attempted kidnapping by two hoodlums. With her voice shaken, her body covered in mud, and her hair a mass of tangles, Shelby faced this well-groomed handsome gentleman and described the threatening evil from the night before. She half-way expected him to throw her out by her scruffy appearance.

"I slept in the woods under a tree last night until daylight," she uttered through labored breathing.

With his eyebrows raised, the man considerately listened to the young woman in front of him and shuddered at the sketch of horror she described. After insisting she be seated close to the fire, he offered a white linen handkerchief and brought a glass of water from the kitchen. Shelby remained standing to avoid transferring mud to a white leather couch and hesitated to take his white monogrammed handkerchief until he insisted. The man, then, immediately called for his housekeeper.

"Ms. Maude?"

"Yes, Mr. Chris?"

"Please come quickly.

"This young lady has endured a traumatic experience. She needs our support."

Maude Hopkins, a mature lady, dressed in a black and white uniform, placed her hands over her mouth, shocked at the sight of the young lady standing before them. The brief explanation of Shelby's nightmare horrified the housekeeper as well.

"Please take care of her, get her clean, warm clothes and treatment for those cuts and bites. She survived a night of horrendous terror and may need a doctor.

"Ms. Maude will take care of you," he said sympathetically.

Shelby accepted his invitation after a brief hesitation and followed Ms. Maude up a winding staircase to a luxurious bedroom with a connecting bath.

The housekeeper gestured with a gentle European accent, "Here, Love, let me help you," her eyes filled with motherly compassion. At the same time, she examined Shelby's wounds to determine whether to send for a doctor.

"I laid towels out for you in the bathroom and clean clothes, love. No doubt, a long, warm shower will do you a world of good."

"I don't want to impose," Shelby objected.

"You are not imposing, dear. You'll likely hurt Mr. Chris's feelings by not accepting his hospitality. You can trust him. He is a kind and caring man."

"Thank you. I will make sure to return these clothes," Shelby's stuttered.

Ms. Maude merely turned her head from side to side in disgust at anyone responsible for such a handsome young lady's trauma. She politely left Shelby alone after supplying her with proper medication for her wounds.

Shelby stood in the shower, weak and trembling. Her body involuntary twitched, sensitive to soap and warm water spraying over her injuries.

"My body compares to a battlefield," she grimaced.

She tended to her wounds and dressed in a soft pink jogging suit and white canvas shoes laid out by the housekeeper. While sitting at the dressing table and tying her clean hair into a ponytail, she thought about the clothes Ms. Maude laid out and to whom they might belong, the lady of the house, perhaps a daughter, or maybe a maid.

Shelby's keen eye for decorating and design called attention to the room décor.

"This bedroom has feminine touches unlike the rooms downstairs," she mumbled aloud and focused on the ornately carved, four-poster bed.

"The bed is a decorator's delight. The quality is skilled artwork, possibly imported. The delicate pink coverlet and quilt in pastels enhance the wood grain," she said aloud, her voice still shaken. "The window treatments include valances of the same hues as the bed covers."

Shelby appreciated the influence of design and other highlights as she gazed around the room. An elegant Persian area rug embraced a polished hardwood floor. Two accent chairs, upholstered in pale-yellow fabric, faced a small rectangle glass-top coffee table creating an intimate seating arrangement. The wall featured impressive oils, notably a portrait of a strikingly beautiful lady centered above the bed. The face of the woman, complimented by delicate background hues of pink and white, glowed with ethereal beauty. Her pale-yellow hair and an off-the-shoulder gown of pearly pink heightened the intensity of the subject. Shelby stood admiring the painting, grasping every detail. She had painted with oils since the fourth grade and quite art knowledgeable.

Is this a portrait of the lady of the house? Shelby wondered.

A dressing table, void of toiletries, suggested the room was uninhabited. Shelby gazed admiringly at the splendor of the place before the housekeeper returned to attend to any further needs.

"Ms. Maude, the shower helped. I feel like a human being again. Thank you for everything."

"Oh my, don't you look different," the housekeeper said, smiling proudly as the two descended the stairs. They entered the great room where scents of burnt embers from a glowing fireplace, and fresh bakery goods from the kitchen filled the air. Shelby found her host lounging comfortably on one of two white leather sofas, his arms outstretched over the back. To her surprise, her heart fluttered with excitement when he rose to greet her with a welcoming grin. She appreciated how his work clothes fit his frame so perfectly. He is not your average farmer, she thought, smiling. She gave regard to his strong jaw, his thick, dark brows, and eyelashes framing deep brown penetrating eyes that sparkled with hints of green and gold circling dark pupils. His coloring contrasted his white hair and his stately demeanor. Powerfully impressive.

"Well now, forgive me the liberty of saying, but you are a most handsome young lady with the mud gone. Is it acceptable for me to call you Shelby?" he asked, and with a broad smile, disclosed pleasure in realizing her attractiveness and engaging charm.

"Thank you. Yes, of course. Please call me Shelby, Mr., er," Shelby paused, a little self-conscious having not remembered if he had introduced himself.

"I didn't choose to be rude at your arrival," he explained. "I didn't expect to find a pretty young woman so lost and frightened in my house. My name is Christopher Standish," he said, "I live here with Ms. Maude and with Jason. I've sent for Jason to help remove your vehicle from the trench before we call the authorities. You will meet him shortly."

Suddenly, Shelby gasped and jumped to her feet at the sight of two male figures rushing by an outside window.

"We employ several hands who work with the animals and take care of the farm. They are completely trustworthy," Standish calmly explained, aware of her sudden fear.

As if on cue, a younger, splendid-looking young man entered the room. Standish introduced him to Shelby as Jason. Standish explained about her abandoned vehicle and gave Jason a brief account of the trauma she faced the night before. Jason reacted to the description of Shelby's traumatic experience with the same alarm and heartfelt compassion as Standish and Ms. Maude.

"I'm so sorry, Ms. Shelby. You suffered such pain," he said.

"Jason, I want you to work on getting this young lady's vehicle out of a muddy trench."

Standish turned toward Shelby, "Jason is completely reliable, and someone I depend upon and trust with my life."

"Sure, I'm happy to," Jason beamed at the introductory comment from Standish. "Tell me where I can find your vehicle, Ms. Evans."

Like Standish's modest demeanor, Jason wasn't close to resembling Shelby's mental image of farmers where she grew up. She estimated his height at slightly under six feet, minutely shorter than Standish. His teeth shine like a movie star's, she thought, and his eyes, blue as a clear summer sky. His silky blonde hair streaked with silver highlights is most certainly a designer cut. I'm sure neither of them chews tobacco as some of the farmers in the county where I grew up. She facetiously thought to herself.

"Please call me Shelby," she offered, "I'm not sure how far away from here it is, but if we head south, we'll find it on the northbound side off the road and sunken into a turbid river of mud."

Shelby smiled timidly at both men and prepared to gather her soiled clothes to discard them, only to find Ms. Maud had attempted to salvage them as well as possible. She graciously thanked them for their hospitality and readied to leave with Jason.

"Mr. Standish, I appreciate so much how you, Ms. Maude, and Jason made me feel at home. I am fortunate to have found this house. You saved my life."

"It's Chris. We're pretty informal here," he said with a voice, powerful, yet soothing as a halcyon sea.

"Ms. Shelby, I want you to remain here until Jason retrieves your truck," he said. "He will take some of the farmhands with him, "and without a pause, Standish spoke politely with a commanding tone, "If you will, please, give him your keys," he beckoned his hand. "You may want to write something nice about me in your newspaper column," he joked.

Shelby hesitated, undecided, but circumstances forced her decision. She understood by his actions he was comfortable giving orders.

She complied with Standish's order and handed her keys to Jason. She trembled, reliving her experiences from the night before, and humbly uttered a thank you to her host.

Shelby sat on one of the sofas across from Standish and nervously repeated her appreciation for the kindness and hospitality to her new acquaintances. After several minutes, talking to Standish and watching his peaceful mannerisms, she soon relaxed. He engaged her in casual conversation about his home, her family, her hometown, and her job before moving to Kentucky. Aside from being a magnificent specimen of the male species, she believed a nobler man didn't exist than Christopher Standish. In her observation, he was the epitome of entirety. The two of them settled in a comfortable, get acquainted mood when to her surprise, Standish removed a long white wig from his head and revealed short, flawlessly styled, umber brown hair. She realized she was facing a youthful, spirited younger man than what she had initially perceived.

"Oh!" She exclaimed, intoxicated by his comely image. He didn't appear more than ten years older than Jason.

"I wear the wig when I work outside. It keeps bugs off my neck," Standish smiled.

What are these two handsome men doing in this area? She wondered.

Ms. Maude entered the room with hot tea, fruit, and a tray of freshly baked breakfast cakes. She and Standish shared a glance, and both chuckled at his comment about the wig. Shelby, feeling more at ease inside the stranger's home, began to share the beginning of a comradery friendship with her new acquaintances over breakfast.

"This is such a unique and wonderful home," Shelby said, recognizing the quality of objects around the room. Standish described some of his artifacts, including a painting of the Basilica he had recently bought while on a visit to Italy when suddenly, Jason's interruption brought discouraging news.

Thirteen

"***Miss Shelby, we*** located your truck. It is leaning over on its side. Vandals severely damaged it. I want photographs before pulling it out of the mud," he dispiritedly told her. "They broke the windows and took the radio." I'm not sure what else.

"Oh, no!" Shelby gasped. "I left another set of keys to the house and office in the glove compartment."

Standish took charge and lifted the phone. "We'll notify the authorities and evaluate the damage," he said.

From her side of the conversation, Shelby overheard him speak to someone at the police department with whom he seemed well acquainted. He decidedly related an account of the abduction attempt and description of the two hoodlums as Shelby described, and listened for a response.

"Thank you, Tom, she is safe now, but what a nightmare this young lady endured. I trust you will want to get a team together and conduct a thorough investigation. I'm concerned the culprits have keys to her home and newspaper office and will remain a threat to her. Miss Evans will phone the newspaper office and give Sam a heads up."

After his conversation with Sheriff Tom, Standish settled the phone and turned to Shelby, "I want you to stay as our guest until the culprits are in custody," he said. "Sheriff Tom and his deputies will investigate and determine a safe time for you to return home."

"I appreciate your invitation, but I truly cannot accept," she said with a firm voice. "I cannot impose further upon your kindness."

Standish continued to speak as if oblivious to her resistance, "Jason will take you home to get clothes and personal items. If you are here with us next week, we will take you to your job. I will hear of it no other way," he said as if giving her a direct command. Her memory as a child surfaced as if she was safe at home with her parents. She appreciated the protection Standish offered. His kind words lightened her worried mind, but she stammered to decline.

Once Shelby called her editor, Sam Shoney, Standish asked to speak to him. The two men confirmed it best she be protected at the farm until the culprits were behind bars.

"I am rewarded with another female in the house," Ms. Maude quickly reassured her. "Besides, once Mr. Chris makes a decision, you may as well give in."

Shelby, so taken by the hospitality of total strangers, their controlling authority, and determined efforts to protect her, found it useless to protest. She observed each one. These beautiful people are disallowing me to reject such a generous offer. In some strange way, she concluded, she should stay, and humbly accepted.

Jason smiled, graciously offered his arm to her, and escorted her to a nearby garage to a shiny black, late model BMW sedan. Both were silent on the way to her cottage until they came upon the farmhands who were taking pictures of her truck. She shivered in horror at the destruction, realizing the viciousness of the two depraved villains from whom she escaped.

"Thank God you are physically fit enough to have gotten away from those two," said Jason.

"I dread what the consequences would have been if they had gotten hold of me," she said after collecting her composure. "Also, I wouldn't have met such nice people as you and everyone at the farm," she smiled.

Shelby slyly peeked at Jason while he drove. He was strikingly familiar to her, but she decided he might remind her of someone she had seen while she was a reporter in Chicago. Shelby thought about the lifestyle in which Jason and Standish lived, the contrast between their distinct cultural backgrounds, and of their affluence compared to the local environment. They are health-conscious, and their grooming associated with a farming community? What am I missing? Are they vacationing? They aren't the typical farmers one expects to see in this area. Whoever they are, I am fortunate to have found them, she admitted.

Shelby gazed at farm homes along their drive into town. Fields of corn and scenic landscapes sparkled with promising sunshine. Scattered grazing cattle, sheep, and horses dotted the farmland. After reaching Main Street, she, and Jason rode by several storefronts. One advertised clothing and yard goods. A corner grocery stood adjacent to Willoughby's' Hardware. Shelby snickered silently at a diner across from Sheriff Tom's' office, wondering if their menu included doughnuts for the deputies. A half dozen school-age children played handball in the local park, while a young couple walked along a jogging path behind a baby stroller. Trees on Shelby's street, oak, and elm, interspersed with weeping willows bordered sidewalks in front of well-tended homes, enhanced by beautifully manicured lawns.

Jason parked at the curb near a large elm tree in front of Shelby's two-bedroom, clapboard cottage, tastefully painted pale yellow with white shutters.

"I will go in with you in case anyone has used your keys."

"Thank you, Jason. I appreciate it."

Gratefully, the door remained intact and locked. However, upon entering the two found gratification of believing no one had broken into Shelby's home was short-lived.

"OH! NO!" Shelby shouted.

A lack of order in the living room startled her, and when she entered her bedroom, Shelby's body stiffened. She gasped and pressed her hands to her paled face. Jason abruptly stopped behind her and raked his fingers through his hair in disbelief. Clothes and scraps of food scattered around the room and empty food cartons strewn about her rumpled bed told the story. Drawers toppled upside down, had spilled the contents. Muddy shoes trampled her under-garments. Closets emptied, and clothes in heaps on the floor caused chills down Shelby's spine. Personal items and toiletries jumbled in disarray exposed her private life. The medicine cabinet left bare. Mud deliberately spattered over the bathroom floor and walls. The invasion of privacy and destruction overwhelmed her.

"The glove compartment contained another set of keys and my address information on insurance papers," she said, regretfully reminding herself.

"I found the glove compartment empty," Jason said.

A television and computer were missing from the guestroom. In the kitchen, evidence showed the intruders had taken time to raid Shelby's refrigerator. The ice container purposely slammed across the room created a dent in the wall and a pool of water on the floor.

"Evil destruction!" Jason said, sharing her heartache while summarizing the damage. "Don't worry, Shelby. Chris, Ms. Maude, and I are here for support. You won't go through this alone.

"The police are on their way, and after you call your landlord, I'll call the locksmith and make sure all locks are changed. I want you to gather clothes you will need for at least a week," he said.

The two waited for a few moments, and gloomily eyed the damage before Jason broke the silence,

"Shelby, this is an attractive cottage, tastefully decorated. I admire your style. These paintings throughout the rooms are fabulous. Thankfully, the intruders didn't take them or destroy them. You will have to put me in touch with the artist when this is all behind us."

"Thank you, Jason," Shelby said while hastily picking up her clothes and personal items from off the floor.

She accepted his effort to boost her morale but neglected to claim herself as the artist.

After Bonnie, Shelby's landlord permitted her to change the locks, Jason called Willoughby's hardware store and ushered instructions. While the two of them sat silently on the front porch swing and waited for the police. Jason put his arm around behind Shelby and started a conversation to divert her attention and hopefully relieve some of her mental stress

"Have you worked in the newspaper office long? Where did you live before moving here?" Jason's questions continued.

"I lived in Chicago and worked as a reporter and columnist for six years. I expected a safer, quieter life by moving here." They both managed a chuckle.

"My parents live in Madison, Indiana. I love where I grew up and often make time to visit my parents," she said.

"What about you?" Shelby asked.

"I came to the farm a little over a year ago," Jason said. "Before moving here, I lived in California. I came for a brief visit, but once I fell in love with the area, the animals, and especially Ms. Maude's cooking, I stayed longer than I had intended."

Watching Jason as he spoke, Shelby silently reflected the relationship between the two men, Jason, and Standish. Jason's boyish features and coloring were lighter than Standish's. Standish's dark eyes and hair and refined sturdy jaw likened a subtle Mediterranean characteristic. Shelby failed to detect a direct resemblance of the two, except for curious personality similarities, impeccable grooming, and manners.

Shelby listened attentively before asking with the composition of a reporter, "Are you and Mr. Standish related?"

Before Jason answered, the authorities and a clerk from the hardware store arrived simultaneously.

Deputies introduced themselves as Harlan and Jess. Harlan, middle-aged, was a short, stocky man with a gentle smile, bushy hair, thick eyebrows, and big hands, characteristically of what Shelby related to as a jolly grandfather.

I wonder if he plays Santa at Christmas, thought Shelby.

Jess, a younger, tall, and slender man, in his twenties, sporting sideburn, reminded her of Elvis's early years. The two deputies asked questions of both Jason and Shelby and then scrutinized the perimeter while taking photographs. Inside the cottage, Shelby watched as Harlan focused on the kitchen and bathroom for fingerprints. He described to her how the kitchen and bath were prominent places of finding prints.

"Please secure this house with your best deadbolts and chains," Jason directed to the locksmith. "Also, check all windows, make sure they are tight, and please send the bill to Mr. Standish's farm," and with his finger to his temple, "Yes, contact Ms. Evans's boss at the newspaper and confirm to him what has happened. He will want to change his locks as well."

Shelby leaned back, braced against the wall with her arms folded, and listened to Jason's explicit instructions to the locksmith. She supposed, by his demeanor, he was as convincingly effective as Standish. His youthful image dictated immaturity, but Jason exceeded maturity beyond measure.

After the inspection, the police chief arrived and conversed with his deputies. He introduced himself to Shelby as Tom Jeffries.

"We concluded the intruders used keys stolen from your truck, Ms. Evans. No sign of a break-in," Chief Jeffries told her.

He assured her of a thorough investigation and a follow-up report as soon as possible. After putting necessary safety measures in place, Shelby gathered her things as Jason instructed, and the two of them headed to the farm.

"Please give the bill for the new locks to me when it arrives," Shelby told Jason as they drove.

"Chris will take that up with you," he said with a reassuring smile.

At the farm, Jason and Shelby gave an account to Chris and Ms. Maude about the break-in and the precautionary changes.

"Jason, it was a good idea for you to call the locksmith right away. Also, call Bonnie and tell her we want to install a security system." Chris talked over Shelby and directly to Jason.

"Mr. Standish, please," she interrupted, attempting a formal directive. "I can't afford the security system and certainly can't allow you the trouble and expense. You've done more than enough for me. I'm not afraid to stay alone. I may consider getting a dog to alert me if someone is lurking outside."

"Please, Ms. Shelby, I insist. I am a little behind on good deeds. You will help me feel good about myself."

Shelby realized his heartfelt sincerity to help her and fell silent. She would take the matter up with him in the future.

Later, in the kitchen— "Please allow Mr. Chris to help you, love," Ms. Maude said with her motherly British accent, "he can well afford to, and he is happy to have someone to care about."

"What about Jason? Is he a family member?"

"Mr. Jason is considered family. He is as caring, generous, and as kind as Mr. Chris," she replied without further elaboration.

"And as persuasive, I've found," Shelby decisively remarked.

After a delicious dinner, Shelby visited comfortably with her hosts before Ms. Maude helped her settle into the delightfully decorated pink room she had visited before. Lying in a luxurious bed of satin sheets after her frightful ordeal and not having been to bed the previous night, Shelby, feeling safe among new friends, readily welcomed a night of uninterrupted sleep. She quietly murmured questions before drifting off into a much needed, peaceful sleep.

They are so kind, such guardian angels, but mysteriously secretive. Why am I allowed an acquaintance with these exceptional people without knowing more about them?

Fourteen

Sforza family members, Lorenzo and Josef, and their sons, Josef's son, Giovanni, and Lorenzo's sons, Nikki, and Benito, joined the two detectives to coordinate their thoughts. They formed a team, pooled their findings, talked about their suspicions, and planned a scheme of action to find the truth behind Giovanni's death. Weeks passed, nothing of any consequence had developed, and then a former member of the Polizia di Stato, the Italian Police Force, heard of the investigation and contacted Nikki Sforza. The informant, who gave his name as Salerno, told the Sforza family that he had written an accurate account of the recovery of Sforza's body, and how he was instructed by his superior to destroy the document and write another describing evidence of an accidental drowning. Salerno saved the original record predicting an opportunity to one day declare the truth. He claimed that he, a young rookie, and their superior officer, witnessed the gruesome scene at the recovery site.

Two weeks after the recovery of Sforza's body, the young rookie was found in his car, slain, with a bullet in his brain. The gun found at the scene was untraceable, and the death ruled a suicide. No one explained why the fatal shot was fired into the right side of the rookie's head when his family claimed him to be left-handed.

Salerno suspected an officer fired the shot. He described how he had changed his identity, gathered his family, and relocated from Florence to the Southern coast of Italy near the Mediterranean Sea. Salerno was fearful for his family, who, along with him, were in jeopardy of being killed.

"I'm encouraged by this document. It is the first substantial clue," Jack told Chris. "When Salerno became aware of our inquiries, he rallied to bring forth pertinent information. His superior pinpointed precisely where to bring the body to the surface, which initially created suspicion to Salerno. He said the commanding officer instructed Salerno to quickly remove ropes and weights from the victim before notifying anyone. Salerno told how he prepared the original document and hid it in his pocket after his superiors instructed him to destroy the paper and create another. The false report, dictated by the superior officer, omitted an accurate description of how the body was found, bound, and weighted.

Consequently, the court ruled the drowning a tragic accident. Salerno admitted to Guinizelli that he saved the original document because of being distraught over the cover-up behind what he concluded, a murderous plot. Salerno hoped to one day present the initial report to a source who would finally bring the killers of Sforza to justice. When handing over the faded original document to the Sforza family, Salerno asked for anonymity. He saw firsthand the cruelty and threats to other individuals and remained fearful.

"This is a big step," Cravens said, "Guinizelli interviewed Salerno and found him credible. This information is confirmation of betrayal by members of the Italian Police, but without Salerno's testimony and nothing else to go on, it will be difficult to prove. We need facts. Hopefully, some of these people will reconsider and come forward to testify."

Stone and the Sforza family grieved over Giovanni's fateful torture. They devastated over the chilling fact he may have been alive and conscious when placed into the water. They were grateful for the new evidence and hopeful of bringing justice to their fallen brother finally. Chris's involvement to prove the cause of his father's death, whispered among townspeople, exposing his identity as the lost son. Fishers living along banks of the Arno River at the time of the drowning eagerly showed their support by coming forward. Residents who had suspected foul play offered what they remembered about the drowning. A conflict of controversy arose among the community. Those close to the Sforza family disclosed their hostility toward members of the Polizia. They complained to have been misled by provincial authorities and referred to the drowning as a pseudo cause of death. Others, not so well-informed, accepted the incident as accidental.

Friends and family of Gio Sforza described him as a well-liked, hardworking individual, still mourned by his family and friends. Family members believed Sforza's death was a contracted murder plot to separate Maria and Gio, the two lovers. They found the scheme was instigated either by greedy motives of family or by members of the Ballet. Events of so long ago began to resurface as a reminder of the tragedy. The Italian Policemen involved in the murder no longer held positions of judicial authority. They had either retired, moved away, or passed on answering to a higher power.

Pierre Boulud, a French freelance reporter who wrote as a syndicated columnist, heard of the tragedy and succession of incidents while vacationing in Florence. He became intrigued by the mystery and began a search. Boulud interviewed family members, friends, and neighbors of the Sforza family. If indeed, a murder had been covered up by police years ago and resurfaced, it was an opportunity for him to by-line a story. He determined to learn the truth. Intrigued, Boulud began building creative theories based on facts from the concept of secret scheming of crime and cover-up of Sforza's death. He gathered all the information he could muster and embellished the mystery with a hypothesis of two young lovers torn apart by prejudice, professional status, greed, and possible premeditated murder. The story caught the attention of readers, begging for more.

The disappearance of a newborn child thought to have perished but miraculously surfaced as an adult to solve the speculative drowning of his biological father became an imaginative stimulus for Boulud. His investigation led to the ballet company where Maria Villella had performed. Boulud discovered names of controlling investors of the ballet company whose conquering success relied on critical performers and who expected a profitable gain from performances — a possible motive for the killing. Some of those former investors were now deceased or no longer held an interest in the arts. A couple of them, both entrepreneurs, remained actively involved.

Careful not to reveal specifics or accuse individuals by name, Boulud created an outline of how power, the authority, influence, and demands of an overbearing family were all contemplative motives for murder. However, speculation of a crime having been committed leaned toward supporting facts and names of prominent people thought to have constructed a conspiracy. A fact-finding panel of a National law enforcement agency reviewed Boulud's study, which led to reopening the accidental drowning case to establish the validity of premeditative murder. An atmosphere of mystery kept the viewer in suspense.

Boulud received death threats, but his steadfast story-telling power continued to reach the reader's eye. Boulud told of a succession of incidents described by Sforza's family. Dedicated readers hungered for more. He painted grim details of how a young mother, under coercion, gave her newborn son to an adoptive family after the baby's father had drowned. The mother disappeared as well, until much later when photographs of her performing with a Russian ballet began to surface in newspapers.

Boulud's dramatic account of two people viciously torn apart because of loving one another had all the earmarks of an emotional drama fit for the big screen. The intriguing drama became nationally known in Southern Europe and the United States, catching the attention of television programs, such as 24 hours and 20 20. Pierre Boulud joined Cravens' team as an investigative reporter in codetermination to expose the truth.

"Chris? It's Jack. Because of all the probing, public interest, and media coverage, the Surete Nationale, or ministry of Interior, a national law enforcement agency, has officially directed the National Gendarmerie to re-open your father's case to abstract truth from conjecture. Boulud, along with the media, has awakened the entire nation to the story. A request for the exhumation of your father's body is in the works. Your family is becoming famous.

"An administrator working for the police during the time of Sforza's death confessed to Guinizelli he witnessed an agreement between two people discussing a bounty on your father's head. He claimed either your maternal grandfather or an investor of a Russian Ballet Company was involved. It was unclear. We are searching for concrete evidence before making accusations.

"Thanks, Cravens. Good Job! Should I come to Italy?"

"No! Not yet. We need solid proof to expect to solve this case. However, through recent events, new evidence, and notoriety from the media, I am confident the reopening of this case will reveal the truth. People threatened before are coming forward with critical information. Some of those directly involved may have passed on.

"Can you remember anything about your maternal grandparents? Are they still living?"

"Maria's mother passed away when Maria was a young girl. Maria didn't give an account of why she became estranged from her father, and I didn't press her. I recall her father was a former member of the Latvian legislative cabinet when they lived in Riga, the Capital of Latvia. They moved to Moscow when Maria's career centered toward ballet. Her father worked briefly for the Russian government, but it was unclear to me as to what capacity. I failed to locate his whereabouts after our accident. He may live in a retirement home. When I reunited with Maria, she hadn't spoken to her father for some time. She described him as stern, stubborn, and militarized. She called him domineering, combative, and as regimental as a Russian Spetsnaz. If he lived in Moscow at the time of Maria's death, I failed to find him."

"Thanks, Chris, I'll see what I can dig up."

Fifteen

Sun peeped through shutters lacing walls of the luxurious pink bedroom with a jeweled brilliance. Shelby suddenly awakened and jolted in an upright position. Emotions stirred until she quickly recalled the perilous journey the previous day, before safely reaching the farmhouse. She shivered at the memory of having slept under nature's life-preserving tree among unknown critters. Shelby gazed about the room and thought, what a contrast of setting. Chirping sounds of a cardinal from outside the window called for its mate. Shaken and bruised from her injuries but safe and out of danger, Shelby paused, took in deep breathing exercises, and, standing at an open window with her face toward the heavens, gave a prayer of thanks. She proceeded to take her morning stretches before showering and then dressed in a white cotton shirt over black leggings. She pulled on black riding boots, descended the stairs, and listened for activity. There were no voices or movements about the house. The house remained peacefully silent.

"Ms. Maude? Jason? Mr. Standish?" Still no answer. "Where is everyone?" Shelby mumbled. Drawn by the aroma of fresh coffee, Shelby walked further into the deserted kitchen. The spacious kitchen, not an ordinary farm kitchen, suitably equipped to accommodate large groups. The appliances: two stoves, two refrigerators, and two large separate ovens, were the most up-to-date, top-of-the-line, modern equipment known to Shelby. A side buffet table filled with breakfast delicacies: fresh fruit, bagels, juices, and other delights allured her taste buds.

"This appears prepared for a special occasion," she said aloud.

"Yes, indeed!"

Startled, Shelby turned in the direction of a familiar voice. Christopher Standish, fashionably dressed in a casual, custom pair of tan slacks, black linen shirt, and without the wig, was handsomely stylish. Enamored by his presence, she smiled a sunny smile, aware her expression mirrored surprise and predictably a little adoration.

Wow! She said to herself.

"You, my dear, you are our special guest," he said. Ms. Maude prepared this, especially for you. The rest of us awakened at dawn and tended to the animals before eating breakfast. Now, if you will sit and make yourself at home and consume a portion of this food, you will certainly help keep our housekeeper happy."

"This is wonderful. How incredibly nice of all of you."

Chris's generous hospitality, and the warming reception from Jason, and Ms. Maude, all strangers to her, rewarded Shelby's thoughts of humanity.

"I must go into town and take care of business, Chris said. Ms. Maude is shopping at a local farmer's market. She'll arrive home soon. Please sit, enjoy, and make yourself at home."

With a matter-of-fact blend of a request and direct order, Standish bade her a pleasant good-morning and turned to leave. Suddenly, he turned toward her, expecting she may feel a little deserted, and said, "Shelby, I assure you everything will work out regarding your attempted abduction and theft at your home. Above all, we will find out who terrorized you and bring them to justice," he smiled reassuringly, returned her wave, and left her alone.

Shelby wondered what he meant about taking care of business, and why was he so confident about everything working out? What company business does a man of his caliber conduct in this country town? And, on a Sunday, what is open?" He reminded her of a high-ranking aristocrat or patrician.

After a delicious variety of breakfast treats, which Shelby gladly sampled, she began to tidy the kitchen, making room for Ms. Maude's vegetables from the market.

"GOOD MORNING, SUNSHINE! Did you sleep well?" Jason burst through the side door from the corral, loud and full of energy.

Shelby jumped but soon recovered when she saw Jason's bright smile.

"And what are you doing, cleaning up the kitchen? Ms. Maude will give you grief, and us, for permitting you to work in what she insists is her domain," he laughed to soften any harshness his words may have conveyed.

"Yes! I slept like a log and comfortable as a queen," she said humbly. "You are a special family to whom I am eternally grateful."

"We aren't anxious for you to leave, but hopefully the authorities will find the perpetrators and arrest them soon. One thing for sure, you can't leave us until police are confident you are safe in your home," he said.

"Jason, you all are being so nice, taking an interest in someone who is a total stranger. You've gone beyond the call of duty, protecting me. Are there enough local law enforcement authorities equipped to protect people in jeopardy?" she questioned.

"First," he explained, "you quickly became a friend. Secondly, Chris has a degree in criminal law and carries a notable influence on law enforcement and State government. Some respect him as the law, a government figure of importance. Not to make too sharp a point, but he has a lot of clout in this county and resents anyone threatening another. He has taken what has happened to you personally and will use his resources to keep you safe. He advocates justice and is productively involved with local and State authorities against criminal activity.

"I see," she said, unsure of his vague explanation but with her curiosity satisfied for the time being she made a point to change the subject.

"Jason, I left my cell phone at the newspaper office. May I make a call to my parents? They worry if they can't reach me."

"Of course! Please, make any calls you wish. No problem." Jason led her to the parlor phone for privacy before he tactfully exited the house and returned to the barns.

Sixteen

"Hello, Mom?" Shelby's voice struggled for composure.

"Hello dear, so nice to hear your voice, but you sound stressed. Is anything wrong?"

"Mom, I don't want you to worry, but vandals broke into my place. I am staying a couple of days with friends I met in the area. The police advised me to stay away from the cottage until they complete their investigation," Shelby's voice remained forcefully calm and deceitfully reassuring. She hesitated and waited for her mother's response.

"WHAT??" Janet screeched.

As Shelby expected, her mother cried in horror. Steeling her reserve to speak, and with restrained calmness, she assured her parents she was well taken care of and safe. She purposefully omitted details of the attempted abduction and damage to her truck.

Within a moment or two after hanging up, the cheerful voice of Ms. Maude returning from the market rang out. Shelby ran to greet her.

"Here, let me help you with those," Shelby offered with a warm smile. Ms. Maude held back at first but handed over a couple of the smaller bags. The two of them emptied parcels of various vegetables and fresh foodstuffs onto a counter.

"These are wonderful!" Shelby exclaimed. Please direct me where to go for fresh vegetables."

"Oh my! Look at this nice clean kitchen. I'm certain this isn't the good work of Mr. Chris or Mr. Jason," Ms. Maude declared, her hands on her hips.

"Ms. Maude, if I am to stay here and impose upon your hospitality, I intend to help all I can. Trust me," she said boldly, "I grew up on a farm. I can feed pigs, milk cows, take care of the animals, and even muck stalls. Cleaning the kitchen is no problem."

Ms. Maude merely chuckled with a casual shake of her head. The two quickly became better acquainted as they performed kitchen duties together for the rest of the day. Shelby won more favor from the friendly housekeeper as they broke beans and shared recipes. Later that afternoon, Jason came in from chores in time to wash up before dinner. Chris arrived from a trip to Richmond and promptly invited Shelby and Jason to join him for a glass of wine.

"Sheriff Tom has a handle on the break-in at your home, Shelby," Chris said. "Two suspects are now in jail."

"OH? The two who attempted to grab me?" she asked.

"Once we locate and confiscate the garbage truck, additional evidence will surface. Likely, it is the two locals ne'er do wells, a couple of high-school dropouts now in custody. The sheriff is confident he will soon identify the scoundrels who terrorized you.

"Where did they find them?" she asked, feeling a bit safer.

"They were picked up at their homes for questioning and arrested on suspicion of break-ins in a neighboring town. Authorities in both counties are working to settle the case. Keep your chin up," he smiled.

Shelby, Chris, and Jason enjoyed casual conversation at dinner. Ms. Maude's delicious meal consisted of a variety of fruits and vegetables, excluding meat, not always on her menu. When the gentlemen complimented the meal as always, the modest housekeeper quickly shared credit with her delightful assistant.

"By the way, Ms. Shelby, what types of stories are you covering in this area?" Standish asked, "I traveled recently and haven't had the pleasure of reading your column."

"I am interested in writing about business and education, which is my passion. I find this part of the country has a great deal of untapped potential to utilize modern efficiency in some areas. Also, I want to help young students by offering incentives for goals of advancement. I want to give them motive and power to work according to their best ability toward whatever they choose professionally: manual labor, farming, or other business.

"I'm impressed. I'm concerned about education in the area as well. However, much of what you learn by staying here," Standish said to her, his eyebrows raised, "I sincerely trust you will keep under wraps. We trust your discretion."

Perplexed by his solicitous request, she hesitated, squared her shoulders, and began speaking as if on a job interview, "When I started work in Chicago, I vowed not to compromise the honor of any people, and to abide by the rules of regulation. Unless the news is thoroughly investigated, confirmed, and essential to report, I will not submit it to press. A news article is as reliable as the integrity of its reporters and editors."

Shelby spoke with an intrepid boldness, created equally by her sincerity and by an innate guard of defense.

"Editing and follow-up is part of my job. Sam hired me as both a writer and an assisting editor. I am ardently committed to avoiding sensationalism. I assure you I will not submit anything for print unacceptable to you or this household or without your permission."

Chris gave her an approving nod, "Thank you, my dear. I know we can count on you."

Chris quickly began an informal conversation, particularly in praise of Ms. Maude and her dedication, countering any tension presented by Shelby's protective explanation of her devotion to the newspaper and its readers.

"Our Ms. Maude has been with us for many years. We couldn't manage without her. Jason can't keep the kitchen active from the other side of the stove," Chris joked.

"What about the animals housed in the barns? How many are there? Are they here for a special reason, maybe a circus?"

Her curious inquiries caused the two men to laugh out loud before Chris responded, "You might say they are living in a circus of their own. Some performed in the circus. A few appeared in movie productions. Some are here because a family member who had primarily cared for the animal was either deceased or no longer able to care for the animal. We enjoy the animals and keeping them safe," he said.

We enjoy keeping them in a safe place. They have an area in which to roam without leaving a secure boundary. If not for this farm, many would not have survived. The animals are rescue animals, abandoned by circumstances.

Standish opened about his life and life on the farm with more intimate discussions. It was as if he had gained a confident expectation of trust for his houseguest.

"I am closer to God, living near the woods and surrounded by creatures of nature." Chris paused, lowered his eyes as if reminiscing a thought.

"Shelby, if I may?" Jason picked up the slack, "Christopher is doggedly pragmatic in saving and taking care of the underdog, often literally. The animals are a comfort to all of us. Our domestic animals have more freedom. They are free to roam within the confines of the farmland, which includes several hundred acres, at least the ones not considered prey from the wild. The larger animals number over thirty, not including five horses. Two are in foal. The Shepherds are a comfort to all of us, and several cats keep the barns free from rodents tending to eat the food and startle the horses."

"You might enjoy seeing most of the animals, Chris interjected, "By the way, will you consider joining us horseback riding sometime soon?"

"Thank you; I'd like to. However, what comes to mind is, if these animals are tame and here for safety and care, why not entertain the idea of inviting children to pet them, learn about them, maybe on designated days, one day a month? As an educational tool, such as a petting zoo?"

"Ms. Shelby, what you suggest is a terrific human-interest story, but for now, I prefer to keep a low-key persona," Chris said, "Please grant us this for now? he asked."

"Of course, I will not write about them without your consent," she said, curious about how the animals came to the area. She wondered how Christopher Standish afforded such a lavish lifestyle, and why in the country? Shelby pondered on Christopher and Jason and their relation to one another. Both are well educated and polite to a fault. Too, they admiringly reflect respect and admiration for one another, but what is the connection? The question soon chased out of her mind by a larger one. What is Christopher Standish afraid I might uncover?

With hidden secrets destined to become exposed, Shelby's sudden and unexpected visit to the haven with strangers will inherit conflict and last longer than she or anyone had anticipated.

Seventeen

In the evening hours after visiting with her hosts, Shelby realized the tiring effects from the recent events and readied to bid everyone goodnight. Suddenly, a resounding car horn from the drive startled them. The shock of surprise caused Shelby's heart to thump like a cornered rabbit. Jason peered through the shutter before facing Chris. The two men were calmer than Shelby expected.

"Yes! She's here, Jason said, confirming with a subtle edge of disappointment.

Ms. Maude paced determinedly toward the front door as if she too, knew whom to expect. She hesitated before a consenting nod from her employer, then gently unlatched the door. The two men calmly waited. Seconds' later, loud, confident, high-heeled footsteps jarring the tile floor in the foyer preceded a harsh, demanding voice, announcing the arrival of a woman.

"Noah, where are you?"

Without an immediate response, a louder effort made the same importunate inquiry. Shelby, apprehensive over the identity of the newcomer unnerving her new friends, breathed deeply. She eyed the two men with absorbed attention. Both Jason and Chris stood as the visitor emerged into the room, filling the air with a floral fragrance of perfume. A stunning woman, likely in her forties, Shelby assumed, entered the parlor. Her eyes, too blue to be natural, probably contacts, Shelby thought. Her dark hair shone with a glossy shine as lacquered coal and coiled in a coiffure style, depicted a woman of high maintenance. The woman's clothes displayed the taste of a designer. Chris and Jason both responded with a friendly reception. Jason kissed her on the cheek, and Chris justly introduced her to Shelby as Ms. Carlina. However, Ms. Carlina discourteously failed to acknowledge the young woman. Instead, she clamored as a turbulent wind with a boring account of her flight from California. She began relating her distress, discrediting 'a most annoying pilot' who insisted she keeps her seat belt on when she chose to walk through the plane's cabin during what Carlina referred to as mildly turbulent conditions. The conversation centered wholly on her needs and her discomfort. Chris discreetly signaled to Ms. Maude, who promptly responded by ushering Shelby into the kitchen and quietly closing the door. Ms. Maude managed to present a vague version and description of the new guest to Shelby.

"No need to worry, love. She is harmless, just loud."

"Who is she?" Shelby reverted to type as a conscientious reporter, cutting to the chase with pointed questions.

Ms. Maude hesitated while retrieving two glasses from the cupboard. She carefully poured a small measure of cognac into each glass.

"Ms. Carlina visits the farm infrequently," she explained, with what Shelby detected as a slight expression of regret.

"She and Mr. Chris were friends before I came to work for Mr. Chris."

"I see, but who is Noah?" Shelby asked, confused.

"Noah is the name she calls Mr. Chris because of the animals, you know, like the Ark!"

Determined not to chuckle at the apparent cliché, Shelby asked, "Is Ms. Carlina a relative of Mr. Christopher?"

"No, but she might entertain the possibility," Ms. Maude said with a downward curve of her mouth.

Shelby switched her approach, not wanting to appear cross-examining but curiously wanting to know the involvement of Carlina with Standish. Her version of the newly arrived guest brought to her mind, an ill-tempered shrew.

"Is she staying? Should I move to another room?"

"You are welcome to stay where you are, in the pink room, love," Ms. Maude said.

Shelby held back inquisitive questions to avoid invading on the privacy of the household. After visiting with Ms. Maude, she became a little relaxed after the cognac and readied to turn in for the night and retire to the pink room.

"Goodnight, Ms. Maude. I should sleep well tonight," she said, referring to the cognac.

Ms. Maude smiled as if she understood.

Shelby listened to muffled voices from the parlor when she ascended the stairs and reflected on the compounding mysteries surfacing at the farm.

"So much material for a suspense novel. One I am not privy to write," Shelby mumbled.

"Who is this loud, uncomfortable woman? What else will happen here?" Questions clouded Shelby's mind. Fortunately, her determination to get to sleep helped her ignore teeming events competing for her attention. Without rest, Shelby expected little ability to face whatever puzzling enigma might occur in the future. Gratefully, she slept soundly in the quiet room.

Shelby awakened to a stream of sunlight peeping through partially closed shutters and dancing through shadows upon the bedroom walls. After her morning stretches, meditation, and a quick shower, she dressed casually as the day before. She listened for sounds of activity before entering the kitchen, where she found Ms. Maude preparing a bountiful breakfast.

"Ms. Maude, the house is conspicuously quiet. Is anything wrong?"

"Everything is good, love. Mr. Chris and Mr. Jason stayed up late and visited with

Ms. Lana."

"What about Ms. Carlina?" Shelby asked, "Is she a relative, business associate, or family friend?"

"I guess she is a bit of all three, Ms. Shelby," the housekeeper chuckled.

"Good morning!" Standish said as he walked into the kitchen, flashing a broad smile.

"Did everyone sleep well?" he thoughtfully asked, directing his attention to Shelby.

Ms. Maude winked at Shelby as if to say. We'll talk later.

After exchanging a few pleasantries about weather predictions, Standish asked,

"Ms. Shelby, why don't I escort you into town and check in on your place? I understand Sam has insisted you take the rest of the week to recover, and we might find this a good time to check with Sheriff Tom for an update."

"Wonderful!" she agreed, anxious to return home, and prepared to leave behind recent entanglements and mysteries at the farmhouse. Her instant dislike for Lana

Carlina promoted an additional motive to leave.

"I must get organized before I start back to work," she said.

"Fine! We'll leave shortly after brunch, but right now, I want to say hello to the animals. Will you join me for a morning ride?" he asked while adjusting his white wig.

"I'd love to," she said, delighted by his invitation. "Give me a minute to change into my boots."

After Shelby disappeared from earshot, Chris smiled at Ms. Maude, "That young woman brings a breath of fresh air into this farmhouse,"

Ms. Maude simply grinned approvingly.

Eighteen

In mid-morning, Lana supported her intimidating nature by a performing entrance into the kitchen. Her full length, black dressing gown with matching slippers revealed imported silk and the sophistication of a prestigious designer. Her face flawlessly depicted the artistry of her profession. Her perfect hair cropped high on her head like a crown as if it stood propped in a corner all night.

"Good morning Ms. Lana, did you sleep well?" the housekeeper pleasantly asked. Disappointed by her one-person audience, Carlina disregarded Ms. Maude's greeting.

"Where are Cristopher and Jason?" she demanded.

"They're out either riding in the meadow or tending the animals," Ms. Maude said without further explanation. She determined politeness rigidly to the unpleasant woman whom she pegged as a Mrs. Standish wanna-be.

"Oh!" said Lana, assuming Christopher and Jason went riding in the fields together and decisively failed to ask Ms. Maude about the young woman she saw the night before. She sat at the dining table in a challenging pose, her head held high, legs crossed at the ankles, and one hand on her hip waiting for service. Without looking up from a newspaper, Carlina held out a cup in which Ms. Maude poured black coffee, silently comparing the color of the coffee to Carlina's personality.

Lana's gaze focused on Jason when he entered the dining area. "Did you enjoy your ride, dear?"

"I'm riding later. I just finished tending to the animals," Jason responded respectfully, "Chris and Shelby are coming in from a ride. A wonderful day for riding," he said politely.

"Indeed, it is," Shelby answered as she and Standish entered through the side entrance, both smiling.

"Thank you again, Chris. What a wonderful morning ride. Riding one of your horses is a treat after riding my old nag, Duffy. Although I miss her."

Shelby restrained her shock at seeing Lana. Her vision of the newest arrival did not fit what one would expect in a country farmhouse setting. She is as baroque as a circus queen. Is this a modern rendition of the calico apron? Only people in soap operas dress that way in the morning, Shelby thought, or maybe Halloween trick or treaters.

No one commented on Chris's and Shelby's ride together, but the stewed snarl on Lana's pursed lips lingered like pigeon dung. Ms. Maude's broad grin did not escape Shelby when the two exchanged a passing glance.

Ms. Maude had prepared a delightful lunch, but the conversation was not as heartwarming as before Lana Carlina blew into town. Shelby mentioned her anticipation of returning to her home and her job at the newspaper, attempting to bring Lana into a conversation.

"I don't consider reporters worthy of my respect," Lana inauspiciously blurted.

Jason and Chris glared at her, embarrassed by her wanton remark, which was not totally out of character for the bold, sharp-tongued diva. Lana simply disregarded their disapproving glances as she would ignore hisses from a disappointed theater audience.

Shelby remained stoic as if she was unmoved by such rudeness. Lana vied retorts as if striving to outdo a rivalry. She described recent renovations to her apartment in Los Angeles and praised her two, four-year-old German Weimaraner's she raised from pups. The two men politely nodded at Lana's comments and discussed matters of the farm and barn animals. Shelby, a bit uncomfortable after Lana's remark about reporters, proffered appreciation and praise to Ms. Maude and promptly excused herself. She determined to rescind her visit and prepared to gather her things and leave with Chris.

A short time later, with a calculated delay, Lana made her leave of the table and ascended the stairs with her chin held high. She tossed her head with a swift movement over her left shoulder as if leaving her audience in suspense of a final act of production. Lana had created a persona from which she seldom wavered.

"I am escorting Ms. Shelby to town," Chris said to Jason as Ms. Maude cleared dishes from the dining table. "She is hoping her home is in order and safe enough for her to return."

"Why don't I take her?" Jason offered, overflowing with anticipation.

"No! Not necessary," Chris said, winking at Ms. Maude, who understood neither of them favored to entertain Carlina.

"Jason, why don't you take Lana for a ride in the western fields this afternoon?"

Chris suggested," tongue in cheek.

"Sure thing!" Jason said, rolling his eyes.

Chris smiled over his shoulder toward Ms. Maude.

After Chris and Shelby reached the town, Chris parked his car adjacent to the police station, where he reintroduced Shelby to Sheriff Tom Jeffries.

"Tom, don't you ever take a day off? I saw you here on Sunday."

Tom Jeffries represented a family of law enforcement. His father, a retired Sheriff before him, his grandfather, a former prosecutor, now deceased, and Jeffries' son, currently enrolled at FBI Academy in Washington.

"Crime takes no vacation, Standish. Although, thankfully, things are slow. We can focus our attention on the local deviates who created grief for Ms. Evans.

"Ms. Evans, we've kept a good eye on your place since the break-in." Sheriff Jeffries said, "Mr. Standish's people cleaned it up really good. All locks are new, and Jason ordered a new security system."

"I can't thank you enough," she said to both.

"Any leads?" asked Standish.

Sheriff Jeffries directed his attention to Chris while handing Shelby's keys to her.

"A farmer living in the next county recently reported the stolen garbage truck. The two in possession of the garbage truck, Donnie Glasgow, and Billy James Brown from the same county, recently worked for the farmer doing odd jobs. They are not the ones in custody, but we understand all four, connected by association, are members of a gang of miscreants. No doubt, all are responsible for the break-in at the cottage. Until we pick up Donnie and Billy James, we will provide security around the clock for Ms. Evans.

When Chris and Shelby reached Shelby's cottage, Chris left her to unpack while he inspected every corner of her home.

"Please, let me or any one of us at the farm know if you have qualms about staying alone," he said, readied to leave her alone. He gave Shelby a friendly hug and kissed her cheek. He walked away, looked back over his shoulder, and waved to her, reluctant about leaving her to stay alone until the arrest of the two men who accosted her.

Shelby smiled at him and interpreted his mannerisms as ambiguously telling, but then, she thought she might be fantasizing another drama.

A good night's sleep in her bed without worry of burdening others, and distancing away from oppressive remarks from the prima donna at the farm did not arrive too soon for Shelby. She breathed a sigh of relief with a new alarm system and locks. The sight of a police car on patrol compounded her sense of security enough to sleep peacefully through the night.

Shelby awakened at 6:00 am listening to chirping sounds of baby English sparrows high in an elm tree and cuddled in a nest.

"I'm Hungry, she spoke aloud, but what is here to eat? Ms. Maude took such good care of me, it didn't occur to me to go the market," she sighed.

But when Shelby went into the kitchen, "Oh. My goodness!" She held the refrigerator door open, stepped back, and gazed inside. She placed her hand over her mouth in disbelief.

"Ms. Maude, I assume made a list of everything I scoffed down at the farm," she said aloud and stared at fantastic food and drink items, all of which she had enjoyed at the Standish farm.

When Shelby entered her home office, another surprise, new television, and a computer proudly replaced stolen ones. She realized she had not followed Chris when he walked through the cottage to inspect the security.

"Oh, my goodness! He must have slipped over here during the work on repairing the damage. How can I show my appreciation for such kind and generous people? How can I repay them? Was Chris's business in Richmond on Sunday to replace my lost items?" she mumbled.

Nineteen

A lot had changed for Shelby within the last few days. On the way to the office, images of fear, protection, and recovery whirled through her head.

"Shelby, you and Standish gave me a tremendous jolt when you called. I understand you went through a nightmarish time," Sam said, giving serious attention to her when she arrived at the newspaper office.

"Yes, Sam, it was a frightening experience," she said.

"Sheriff Jeffries came by and discussed his concern over what happened to you. You are fortunate to have found the Standish farm. Chris Standish is a Godsend to this community."

"So, I've discovered. The wonderful people at the farm welcomed me as family. Mr. Standish replaced several stolen items without telling me," she said, still amazed.

"I'm not surprised. Not for publication, but Standish contributes to charities and businesses in the area, including the school system, which he has deemed a priority, as I see you have as well. He is a private person as far as his personal affairs.

Sam Shoney, a kind and proper gentleman, a pillar of the community with an impeccable reputation as a newsman dedicated to printing stories written well and proven beyond doubt. A no-nonsense, hardened reporter in New York, Shoney expected to find solace away from a large metropolis, notably known as 'the city where no one sleeps.' Shoney's decision to move escalated after his wife, Betty, fell victim to a mugging in broad daylight in downtown Manhattan. Betty recovered from her physical injuries, but the assault traumatized her, and she remained afraid to leave her home alone. During Shelby's interview for the job, she, Sam, and Betty struck up an immediate rapport. Shelby soon realized the small town of Poa had become a befitting place of shelter to several.

Sam alerted Shelby to contact her parents before his news article scheduled to appear in the paper the next morning since they subscribe to the RECORD.

The headline read: ***Local newspaper reporter escapes kidnapping and severe harm from a pair of unidentified ruffians.***

The article's conclusion ***Sheriff Jefferies stated: "Those who committed this serious offense are recognizably a danger to the townspeople in this county and surrounding county. They will account for their atrocities and dealt with to the fullest extent of the law."***

Shelby's parents, shaken by the alarming news, called Shelby immediately.

"I convinced my parents I'm safe, and there was no need for them to come here. I told them the culprits are likely the ones in custody," she said.

"This town is beginning to become a challenge," Shelby mumbled after walking away.

After Sam's column, Shelby began receiving cards and letters from many well-wishers to whom she expressed her sincerest appreciation. With no significant upsets occurring within the following days, Shelby walked to the high school every afternoon, but as a matter of security, under the protective eyes of a deputy. She continued teaching her journalism class during the summer months.

Schools across the country were on summer break, but schools in Appalachia experienced numerous closings from inclement weather conditions during winter months. Consequently, school board officials voted to keep schools open year-round. Fortunately, by keeping children in school, petty crimes from delinquents remained at a minimum.

Shelby became further acquainted with the principal and teachers and quickly gained respect from students who filled her classroom. She discovered delving into backgrounds of students was a learning experience. Siblings of students, and other school-age children without proper influence and inspiration, failed to further their education and dropped out of high school as soon as possible. A steady increase in dropouts became a significant issue for Shelby and other faculty members. Children dropped out of school due to emotional problems. Some absentees were promoted by parents who deemed it necessary for their child to work to supplement the family income or help with chores. Other students withdrew from school because of a lack of interest and who had continually failed classes.

Friday afternoon, after she returned home from the newspaper office, Shelby received a call from the repair shop, "Ms. Evans, your truck is ready for pick up, or we will deliver it to you."

"Thank you so much, how much is the final bill," Shelby asked anxiously.

"No bill, Ms. Evans, with your deductible paid, your insurance will cover the rest."

"There is a mistake; I haven't paid the deductible," she said,

"No mistake, Ms. Evans, Mr. Standish, dropped by and paid the $1,000.00 deductible.

With a lump in her throat, she thanked him politely, let out a long sigh, and lifted the phone again.

"Ms. Maude?"

"Oh, my dear, we are so happy to hear from you. Are you ok?" The housekeeper asked.

"Yes! I am fine. Is everyone at the farm, ok?"

"Yes! We are all doing well, love. I will get Mr. Jason on the phone. Mr. Chris is away."

"Shelby, you can't guess how often your name comes up," Jason said, delighted she called, "We miss you. Tell me about your week."

She commenced telling him of her journalism class and her plans to instill new academic opportunities for seniors when he excitedly interrupted.

"How about going riding with me on Sunday? We can catch up."

"Yes, I can. I will have my truck."

"Good! We will see you bright and early Sunday morning and expect you to stay for brunch." His cheerful voice was particularly heartening. The two concluded their conversation without the mention of her replaced items and deductible Chris had paid.

"I'll take that up with Christopher Standish," she said aloud after hanging up.

When Shelby entered her freshly painted truck, she realized at first glance, the installation of a new radio and CD player. She assumed they were additional surprises from Chris Standish.

"What have I done to deserve this? These people have adopted me?" she said, shaking her head in disbelief.

In the afternoon, Shelby gave her parents an update on her truck and belongings but carefully omitted telling them of gifts from Chris Standish. What would it suggest to them without having met Standish and the others? Before settling in for the evening, she shopped at the market, caught up on reading, and outlined stories for future publications. Her current stories detailed works in progress in the community and school system. She expressed the importance of education, and in personal editorials, gave credit to those who performed outstanding work in her class of journalism. In a brief paragraph, she graciously thanked Chief Jeffries, his department, and the people in the community for their caring, good wishes after the attempted abduction and break-in at her home.

Twenty

Shelby recalled how Jason and Chris tended to the animals at daybreak and made her way out to the barns early Sunday morning. She noticed the animals eating and discovered one of the horses missing from the stable. She wandered to the back fences and fixedly stared at the vast fields when suddenly, she heard her name called out.

"Shelby, over here," Jason yelled, dutifully filling buckets with fresh water.

"Good morning Jason," she yelled and ran to the barn.

"Chris has gone riding. Maybe we can catch up with him. Another great morning for a ride."

"Yes, it is," she smiled.

Shelby helped Jason with the saddles, and the two of them led the horses to trot toward open fields where the countryside burst with the wonders of nature. The fragrance of wildflowers in the early morning dew, the chirping of birds, the beam of a rising sun, the swish of a horse's tail, everything reminded Shelby of her roots and the farm where she had lived with her parents. She galloped her horse at a fast pace ahead of Jason, challenging him to race.

"SO, YOUR TALENTS INCLUDE RIDING," he yelled to her.

"I GREW UP ON A FARM. I LEARNED TO LOVE ANIMALS, ESPECIALLY HORSES. I WANTED TO BECOME A JOCKEY," Shelby yelled back.

"WOW! YOU WOULD BE A GREAT JOCKEY. YOU RIDE LIKE A PRO. I'D WAGER ON YOU!"They rode together, side by side, absorbed in the peaceful atmosphere and breathed in fresh breezes of open air. Strikingly picturesque hills and valleys sprinkled with colorful wildflowers offered an exciting subject for Shelby to paint. After a short while, Jason guided Shelby to a thicket of small trees by a lake where they stopped to rest and allowed their horses to drink.

"This is a delightful spot. Riding out here brings me so much enjoyment," she told him as they sat on a log facing the water,"I first saw this lake from a distance when I was lost and wandering before I found the farm. It has special meaning to me."

Jason didn't comment. He merely reached over and squeezed her hand, understanding the suffering she had endured.

"I've discovered this is a calm place to meditate and concentrate on important factors of life. The wonder of nature unfolding its deepest beauty is a gift. Chris taught me to ride when I first arrived at the farm. Living here at the farm has opened up a whole new world for me," Jason said.

"You say you lived in California before?" she asked.

"I grew up in California," he said,"I stayed after college because of my close relationship with Chris. He is an older brother and father figure combined. I graduated from college and sought a career before Chris moved to the farm."

"What did you end up doing?"

"I became an actor. Living in the center of a movie producing community, it seemed inevitable, or reasonable at the time. I seized the opportunity, and it paid the bills. After a while, I became disillusioned by the Hollywood scene. I wanted more out of life than the notoriety of films. I yearned to learn about life and who I am instead of pretending to be someone else in films."

He opened up to her. Suddenly, she realized a connection.

"YOU ARE JASON VANCE!" she cried out, "of course, I recognize you now. I wondered why you seemed familiar. I saw a couple of films in which you appeared. My goodness, Jason, you possess such charisma. Your fans adore you. I read where you had taken a temporary break from Hollywood."

"Chris has always been a tremendous influence. He suggested I move out here with him for a while until I figured out what I wanted. I love working on the farm, the animals, and this splendid sanctuary. I love being here next to nature. The slow pace has given me a new perspective on life in general."

"How long have you been here at the farm?"

Before he answered, the sound of hoofbeats vibrated the ground, followed by a floating cloud of dust.

"Hey, you two! Good, you're out and about. Shelby, we missed you at the farm."

"Chris, this girl rides like a pro," said Jason, "Shelby is a ringer. She is a jockey in real-life."

Chris jumped from his horse and embraced Shelby in a bear hug, "Glad you're here," he whispered.

"I'm aware! I rode with her!" he said to Jason.

The closeness of Chris's body bolted through her like a magnetic force of electricity as none she experienced before. She stammered to recover without revealing her telling emotion.

"I have a real bone to pick with you, Mr. Standish," she threatened.

His eyes settled on her with sparkle and a subtle wink. His regarded attention told her it was useless to offer reimbursement for replacing everything she had lost during the robbery and vandalism.

After a given time for the horses to rest, the three of them mounted their horses and raced to the farm where they would greet their cheerful little housekeeper. The downside came when Shelby caught a brief glimpse of Lana Carlina in the doorway, posing a scowled frown with arms folded. She looked like someone slighted, like watching the last cookie disappear, not like someone angered, which prompted Shelby to reach out to her.

"Hello Ms. Carlina, good to see you again," Shelby's ill-received greeting came with a tight lip response from Carlina. Carlina merely flung her head, rejecting the gesture. Shelby saw a wounded pride for having been left alone.

So much expecting a change of attitude from Lana Carlina, thought Shelby. Still, she wondered what could have happened in Lana's life to have caused such anger.

When the group entered the dining room, Lana pulsed a brief stare toward Shelby and quickly turned away. She spoke directly with a chilling bite.

"I'm so glad to be home again," Lana said, sharply enunciating every syllable.

The remark was meant to unleash a reserved dig, set boundaries, and present a strong family alliance as if defending her territory. To Shelby, it was a silent declaration.

Ms. Lana regards me as a rival, how sweet.

But what happened next caused Shelby to almost gasp.

"Oh! I didn't realize you are planning to live here, Mother," Jason's unrestricted words impacted a shocking disclosure to Shelby, who gulped down a swallow of coffee.

Chris interrupted before Lana responded, "Now Lana, you are far too sophisticated for our little country town."

Conversations escalated with the men hanging together and making jokes about watching Lana slopping pigs and engaging in farm life. They made humorous puns describing Lana's polished, urbane style of living in contrast. She gloried in the attention.

Shelby remained silent and wide-eyed, staring at everyone. The unexpected declaration by Lana increased her curiosity with an eager desire to learn more. The word, ***mother,*** pervaded Shelby's mind. Hearing the suggestion Jason is the offspring of such a rude, self-centered woman, wasn't possible.

"Oh!" she said to Jason, "I didn't realize Ms. Carlina is your mother."

Lana refused to bring discredit to herself in any way, and as if on cue for her next performing line, promptly attempted to establish a firm ground.

"Yes, dear," she said with a self-satisfied smirk, "I am family. And Christopher, I suggest you consider spending more time in LA. You can't remain a country hick forever," she curtly added with a sulky pout.

After Lana's remark, both Jason and Chris laughed aloud, expressing their insensibility. They called each other out about how they liked hoedowns and mucking stalls, which brought a smile to Shelby's lips. Lana, familiar with the comradery between the two men, ignored them and soon headed for the stairs in a manner of privilege, unopen to excuse.

Shelby and the men relaxed in the parlor, where conversations shifted to an hourly weather forecast and Shelby's work week ahead until Shelby decided to leave. She

thanked them for a great time riding on the range, Ms. Maude, for the delicious meal and prepared to leave. Jason jumped up to escort her to her truck, but Chris intervened.

"Now, don't be a stranger," he said when they reached her truck. He politely kissed her cheek and did not comment after she made another unsuccessful attempt to offer repayment to him for favors, he provided after her break-in. Shelby peered over her shoulder and waved to Chris, still stunned at the realization of Lana Carlina as Jason's mother.

"***Mother***," Wow! I can't get the word out of my head," she said aloud.

Shelby accepted riding invitations a few times after work and on Saturday with both Jason and Chris but declined requests for Sunday brunch, telling them she needed time to catch up with her writing assignments. The truth, she didn't favor spending time with the ill-tempered Lana, who expected every audience to kowtow before her.

When she and Jason talked alone, Shelby mentioned to him, "Jason, I detect Ms. Carlina has taken a particular dislike to me. Have I done anything to upset her?"

"Not at all. Lana doesn't like herself. You will learn to take her with, what Chris has said, 'A grain of courage,' he said with a chuckle.

Twenty-One

Sheriff Jeffries, a regular visitor at the newspaper office, dutifully kept Shelby up to date on all issues pertaining to the suspects. He reassured her of the safety measures put in place and the continuation of his deputies standing guard.

"Ms. Evans, in light of new evidence, we are providing you with 24-hour protection until these hoodlums go to trial. We must avoid repercussive out-lashes by any of their friends or family members. We cannot take chances."

"Thank you, Sheriff, but I'm sure I will be fine. My home is secure with the locks and security system, and I won't wander along a country road after dark any time soon."

"Nonetheless, until we interview families of the suspects and investigate their friends, we aren't taking any chances. It is our duty to protect you."

"Yes, Shelby," Sam said, agreeing with the sheriff.

In the following days, Shelby's awareness of the deputies' constant presence gave her peace of mind, with little privacy.

"They are everywhere," she told her parents, who breathed a sigh of relief.

Shelby remained close to her friend, Kate, principal of the high school, whom she trusted as a confidant. On Friday afternoon after classes, Kate commented, "Shelby, I hope you won't mind me asking, but is someone close to you, a friend or beau, perhaps someone you can invite for an extended visit? It's wise for you to have someone stay with you until the trial is over for your safety."

"My itinerary has become a tour guidebook and challenge for local law enforcement," she laughed. "I wouldn't want to endanger anyone, and I haven't dated since my breakup with Tony. I probably wouldn't want to start town gossip by having an affair while law enforcement follows my every move. They both laughed, considering the dutiful eye of the law preventing her from having a love interest.

"Of course, we face another fact of having no prospects," Shelby interjected.

"What about out at the farm?" asked Kate, anxious to protect her friend, and somewhat curious.

"Kate, if you are attempting to play cupid, you've no shot at the farm. You will have to take your bow and arrow elsewhere. Christopher and Jason are both handsome, wonderful men, but I detect no suggestive indication of interest except sincere friendship. Besides, Ms. Lana Carlina, the wicked witch from the West, is using her magical powers to prevent either of them from getting close to any woman, especially me. Jason is her son, and Lana may have a romantic interest in Chris. I haven't figured it out. The farmhands are friendly and congenial. Most enjoy happy lives with families in tenant houses. And Jason, Jason is more of a younger brother figure to me."

"Well, my dear Shelby, you are indeed, a rarity as an eligible young woman in this part of the country. I can't visualize you with any of the local villagers," she declared with tongue in cheek.

Suddenly, a sound from Shelby's cell phone broke into their conversation.

"Shelby, its Chris. Are you available to come out to the farm this evening, say around 5:30?"

"Of course, Chris, I'll be there," she replied, unable to hide her broad smile and trace of color on her cheeks when she turned toward her friend.

"See you tomorrow," Shelby waved, ignoring Kate's inferring suggestion and devilish grin.

"What does he want?" Shelby mumbled. "He sounded serious. I look forward to seeing him, Jason, and Ms. Maude, but I'm not warm and fuzzy about another reunion with the charming Ms. Carlina."

Shelby hurried home to change into an outfit befitting for the farm when her attention diverted to a blinking light on the phone. She listened to a short message and quickly responded.

"Sheriff, this is Shelby Evans returning your call. Any news?

"Yes! Ms. Evans, as we predicted, friends of the bad boys who terrorized you, acquainted with their kind, attempted to break Donnie Glasgow and Billy James Brown out of jail. The culprits slipped away, but information gathered from a relative of one of them alerted us to keep a watchful eye. They vow to keep you from testifying. I hope you are willing to put up with my deputies a while longer," he said.

"Sheriff, what are chances for the trial to move to an earlier date?"

"This is another thing we are working on. We must obtain enough evidence to prevent the unexpected release of the suspects before presenting it to a prosecutor. We're awaiting the arrival of a federal agent to investigate your attempted kidnapping. The same two suspects are under suspicion for other abductions in the area. Ms. Evans, these are career bad boys, and we want as much ammunition as we can muster to put them away for a long time before we take premature steps leading to mistakes.

"I understand, Sheriff, she said.

"At Mr. Standish's request, I am sending a deputy to your house to escort you to the farm this evening."

Shelby embraced the concerns of law enforcement. However, she distressed over miseries and inconveniences she effectively caused everyone.

"If only I had not taken a tour of the countryside that fateful night," she moaned regretfully.

On the ride to the farm, Deputy Harlan boasted to Shelby, his daughter, a student of Shelby's, greatly benefitted from her journalism class.

"My daughter, Jennifer," he proudly told her, "has developed a passion for writing and is eager to go to college. You made an impression on her and my entire family as well," he said.

Shelby's broad smile spoke her appreciation. "Thank you so much for telling me," she said, pleased her efforts made a difference.

Twenty-Two

At the farm, Jason eagerly ran out to greet Shelby as the Harlan drove away.

"Jason, what is so important for Chris to request me to come out to the farm this afternoon?" she asked.

"I'll let him get with you," he said, taking her arm. "He didn't say much to me."

She recognized his evasiveness but declined to comment.

At the house, Shelby predictably received a friendly welcome from Chris, a heartwarming hug from Ms. Maude, and a grim nod and an unyielding determination from the distant Ms. Carlina. Ms. Maude had prepared a place setting for Shelby, who graciously accepted the dinner invitation. After dinner, in the absence of the ever-disappearing Lana, Shelby talked informally in the parlor with Chris and Jason. Suddenly, the conversation abruptly ended. Chris reached for Shelby's hand. He led her to the garden without saying a word. The two sat on a stone bench framed by a wooden trellis supporting growing vines of white tubular flowers. A light fragrance of honeysuckle filled the mild evening air. Red rose bushes encompassed a portion of the garden, providing a blanket of charm to nature's beauty.

Whatever is he going to say? Shelby wondered, and when?

"Shelby?" Chris said, then gave a long sigh and paused. The sobering sound of his voice unnerved her.

"Shelby?" he repeated, "I am requesting you move into the farmhouse for an undetermined length of time," his voice depicted a sudden seriousness and sense of danger to Shelby.

"Sheriff Tom and I investigated these hoodlums. Family members say they are out of control and suspect they have developed an inner circle of crime. Two of them are under suspicion of being linked to the disappearance of two young women from a neighboring county. The women are still missing after two years," he raised an eyebrow and gazed into her eyes with determined reverence. "I would not alarm you without good reason. Law enforcement will try and keep a vigil on them but haven't enough substantial evidence for an arrest warrant.

"Since you came to my doorstep lost and frightened," he said. "I vowed to protect you. Please allow me, allow us to care for you. With our security at the farm, Sheriff Tom and I decided it will be safer for you to stay here for a while."

She couldn't help but remember how easily she walked into his house undetected when she was so desperate but said nothing.

He tenderly held her hands in his and, with a steady gaze, waited for an answer. After a moment's hesitation, she spoke softly, "I didn't anticipate all that had happened," she said ruefully. "Coming to this town to help make a positive difference for children and the community is important to me. I am anxious to get to work and do my job."

Shelby listened to Chris's words of caution but was hesitant to accept his offer. "Chris, I am profoundly moved by your offer, but..."

Before she said anything in protest, he spoke, "Allow us to help keep you safe," he pleaded. His eyes focused on hers as he gently held on to her hands.

Shelby gazed at the protective sincerity in his eyes and remained silent until Jason's determined voice interrupted.

"Yes, Shelby, please take Chris's offer. You can teach me to ride like you."

She smiled at Jason, tears streaming over her cheeks, "Jason, your riding is better than mine now. You ride as if chased by desperadoes in a Western movie."

The two men shifted to laughter in an encouraging and uplifting mood putting Shelby at ease.

"Ok, it's settled," Chris said. "You will move in here tomorrow. A deputy will post by your door tonight, and Jason will bring you here after work tomorrow." Chris spoke with authority but waited for her confirmation.

I don't suppose Chris or Jason will give up. I have little alternative but to accept their generous offer, she determined.

"Thank you," she said reverently.

With Chris's knowledge of earlier unsolved crimes linked to the same two who attempted her kidnapping, threats of further danger terrified her. However, later at night, while at home alone, she questioned her decision to move to the farm and subject herself to recognizable enmity from the sassy bark of Ms. Lana Carlina.

Twenty-Three

Aunt Gina called in midmorning of June twenty-nine to give Chris an update on family and to wish her nephew a Happy Birthday.

"Thank you, but how did you know my birthday?" he asked her.

Your friend, Jack Cravens, told me. He is doing a tremendous undercover job. You share the same birthday as my dear brother, your father. We are delighted to find out for sure. It is an omen of good fortune.

"You are so kind, Aunt Gina. Please give my love to the family. I look forward to seeing all of you on my next visit," he said.

No sooner did Chris return the receiver; he answered a call from Jack Cravens.

"Jack, in talking to my Aunt Gina, she said you found my father and I share the same birthday. The coincident is ironic."

"Yes, but the other news is more interesting.

"Two officers who participated in the recovery of Giovanni's body have volunteered information leading to conspiracy in a premeditated murder. They are retired from the local police station and have enthusiastically cooperated in our investigation. They harbored guilt for over three decades but said nothing because of threats to their lives, lives of their families, and threats of losing their jobs. Their stories, word for word, corroborates with Salerno's statement to Guinizelli. "The other information, I dread telling you," Cravens said.

"What is it?" Chris asked his friend.

"According to another informant, Pia St. Vincent, who witnessed the transaction from an open window at the Florence police station, a man, identified as Richard Villella, was overheard talking to an officer in the ally outside the station. St. Vincent watched and listened as the man reached into his pocket, pulled out a picture of Sforza, gave a description of his work habits, and passed an envelope printed with an inscription of an amount of money agreed upon to dispose of the target. St. Vincent, a member of the gendarmeries, relayed what she overheard to her superior. He rewarded her by threatening to release her from duty and kill her family if she repeated the account. St. Vincent's statement is substantial evidence of the murder of Giovanni Sforza. The crime, committed by the police, was paid for by your grandfather."

"This is dreadful news," Chris said, "Maria likely discovered information implicating her father, which must have been terrible for her. Her opinion of him while growing up was likely unfavorable, to begin with.

To imagine a blood relative of Maria's and mine capable of murder is incomprehensible to me. Maria didn't talk about her family much. She was a young girl when her mother died and practically abandoned by her father, who left her with sitters. She later opted to distance away from him.

"Richard Villella no longer lives in the area where Maria told you she once lived, but he is alive and living in Moscow. Guinizelli located his address."

"What is next?" Chris asked.

"I guess the question is, will you want to pursue this further? I haven't given all the information I've gathered to the prosecutor in

Florence, but regardless, the case is re-opened. What I've found is knowledge for anyone to discover if taking the time. Three informants are willing to talk to us but remain reluctant to go to the authorities. They continue to fear threats and consequences from those who were directly involved.

"Chris, I remind you, if this man is proven to have murdered your father, we are leading toward the arrest of your biological grandfather," Cravens said.

"Wait until I talk to my family in Florence and Rome first," Chris said.

"Sure thing! I will wait to hear from you."

"At any cost, we must get to the truth of what happened. I need a little time to sort out what I've learned," Chris said to Cravens. He dwelled on his conversation with Cravens for a couple of days before calling his cousins in Italy.

"Josef, I received information implicating my maternal grandfather as the person responsible for my father's death. I want to explain the details up to this point and would appreciate your input and ask you to discuss this with Lorenzo, Aunt Gina, and the others before I ask Cravens to contact authorities."

Chris described the findings from the detectives to Lorenzo and Aunt Gina on a conference call and listened for their input.

"Christopher, dear, why don't you visit this grandfather of yours in Moscow? Introduce yourself to him and listen to what he has to say. Regardless of the outcome, you need to pursue this for you. He needs to face you, as well." Everyone agreed.

"Aunt Gina, you're right. I must follow this through. We have come too far not to cross every avenue and lift every stone, so to speak." After they said their goodbyes, Chris sat in silence for several minutes.

After dinner at the farm, everyone gathered around the dining room table to sing happy birthday to Chris. Ms. Maude, who had yet to forget anyone's birthday, baked the most delicious Italian crème cake Shelby had ever eaten. For one precious night, Lana had put on her best performance of good manners and opted to enjoy the evening. Too bad they were not' giving out Oscars, Shelby thought.

Twenty-Four

"Shelby has accomplished a great number of achievements in a short while," Sam Shoney boasted to his wife about his new assistant. "She is teaching a journalism class every afternoon at the high-school and becoming a well-noted and respected figure of our community. I don't want her to become discouraged. I have some ideas I want to discuss with her about expanding the paper."

"Wonderful! Her presence brings a ray of sunshine into the room," Betty replied.

"What? You mean I don't radiate sunshine?" he playfully chuckled.

The next morning at the office, Sam and Shelby enjoyed a second cup of coffee while he inquired about her well-being and life out at the Standish farm, which she approached delicately and discreetly.

"I'm getting a lot of work done at a desk Mr. Standish provided for me. I am riding a lot now while I'm staying at the farm, and most of all, I am enjoying the food Ms. Maude prepares. Honestly, Sam, she dotes on everyone, what an angel."

"More importantly, you are safe," Sam commented.

"Shelby, I have contemplated a new project, a special assignment to take your mind off past circumstances and to give us momentum. You are doing a great job at the school, and your editorials exceed commendably. You give more than I expected from anyone. I am indebted."

"Thank you, Sam. Other than the hoodlums we're dealing with now, a few complaints about barking dogs, domestic issues, and obituaries, the sheriff hasn't much for me to report."

"What are your thoughts about us starting another column? A series of governmental political issues, for instance?" he asked. "It has come to my attention by reading your articles on education and politics; some people in this community don't understand what they are voting for when they vote if they vote. I may ask you to travel to Washington and other places for interviews. The two of us can expand this little paper with a public interest campaign of knowledge. I respect your input."

Sam waited for her response.

Shelby remained silent for a moment and then spoke confidently, "A need to educate people in this community is an essential goal for me. I am open to anything we can accomplish as reporters or concerned citizens to help children reach a higher level of education. I'm all for inspiring adults to set goals for themselves as well. If parents set higher standards, they will become better role models for their children. For instance, I have learned of a hamlet of homes a few miles from here in the hills where families, most related in some way, are left alone in a region where poverty is king. They have little interaction with people outside their colony, not sharing common interests. They fail to send their children to school, proclaiming to homeschool them. From my understanding, many of these people, if any, are ill-equipped to school their children.

"I want to learn about them. Are the people in those hills forlorn of hope? Are they feeling neglected, abandoned, deserted by the townspeople, or is it a matter of nescience? In a sense, what is their obstruction to progress? It's a wonderful idea to indoctrinate political education, of which I am in favor. My idea is, by providing everyone within our community an equal opportunity of education and fundamentals in schooling, health, and everyday living, it is an important place to start."

"My dear?" he beamed, "This is one time I am patting myself on the back for hiring someone smarter than me. I am not privy to this village and pride myself on being one nosy newspaperman. How did you acquire this knowledge?"

"I developed a friendship with teachers at the high-school and Kate Morley, the principal. Kate has kept me up to speed on what students tell her. You can learn a lot from children," Shelby told her editor.

"Indeed, you can," he agreed. "How can we propose to find out about this village, get closer to the people, and find useful ways to free them from poverty? What else has Ms. Morley learned? See what she can find out. The story has earmarks of an excellent human-interest piece, and importantly, an opportunity for the community to unite together and get those children the education they deserve. "

"I would like to visit their homes and interview some of them," she said. "Perhaps we will find what they are experiencing and solutions for some of their problems. First, we must know what the problems are"

"We'll investigate first," Sam replied. "I don't intend to put you in harm's way. You've been through enough."

"People in the area may not welcome Law enforcement," she said. "Rumors of moonshine and other behavioral crimes, including incest, as part of their lifestyle have surfaced over the years. However, these are mere accusations, not proven facts. I will talk to Kate tomorrow and ask her if she can provide additional insight from the children. It is difficult to predict the number of school-age children who are living in that abstract environment without proper guidance. I want to discuss this further with you."

"We'll pursue this, but right now, your ride with Jason has arrived."

Shelby ran out to meet Jason and found him dressed up in dress pants and a white designer shirt. He was the image of what she perceived as a model in 'Vogue for Men'. His usual fashion of sport included blue jeans and golf shirts when not working in dungarees.

"Jason, you look terrific, what's the occasion?" Shelby asked him.

"Jason, a little embarrassed, proudly responded with a huge grin, "I'm going on a date with a young lady from Los Angeles. I'm picking her up at the local airport. She is staying at Jeremiah's Lodge."

"I'm familiar with Jeremiah's Lodge. I stayed there when I first came to town searching for a place to live," Shelby said. "What a marvelous setting, high on a hill overlooking the valley with a full stream at the bottom. The lodge brings a fond memory. Tell me, is this a love interest or friendship rekindled?"

"Her name is Sunni Jamison. She is a young actress I dated briefly before coming here. I gave her my forwarding address, but we didn't stay in touch often. Frankly, I am curious as to why she is coming. She surprised me when she called."

"It's good to stay in touch with people from your past, and healthy to interact with peers your age."

"Thank you, Shelby. You are a great confidant. You always give me reasons to think positive thoughts about myself.

"I enjoy Sunni's company. She has a great sense of humor. She's smart, talented, and pretty as well," he said. "I can imagine Lana's reaction. I haven't told her."

Shelby smiled approvingly. When he dropped her at the farm, she gave him a sisterly hug and bade him goodbye before he anxiously went to meet his friend.

Twenty-Five

Owners of Jeremiah's Lodge, Jeremiah, and his wife, Samantha, better known as Jerry and Sam, dressed appropriately for the lodge setting. The couple looked as if they had walked straight out of a Norman Rockwell painting. They greeted their newest guest with a bottle of champagne, as was their custom for vacationers on an extended stay.

After depositing Sunni's bag, Jason and Sunni sat in a suitably decorated rustic dining room. They relaxed in front of a large picture window overlooking lowlands between the hills and gazed at a lake flowing along the valley. They admired evergreens and trees bordering an Olympic size swimming pool and red and white begonias lining a walkway to the pool, adding color to an inviting landscape.

"Jason, this setting is breathtaking," Sunni told him.

"Yes, it is. I'm happy to see you. It has been a while," Jason said, attempting to hide his curiosity about why such an impromptu visit.

"What is going on in your life?' he asked, making small talk.

"I wanted to take a sabbatical before my next movie began production and remembered you moved here. I hope you don't mind my visit?" the young actress asked Jason, not wanting to intrude.

"Of course not. I love seeing you," Jason said.

Jason grew up with actors, attended movie productions in the making, and withstood the evils of paparazzi. He understood the importance of seeking a haven in which to relax during production intervals.

Tell me about the movie and your role. When is the production scheduled?" Jason asked.

"The story is about a young married couple living in a gay community and having second doubts about their sexuality after they become acquainted with gay couples," she said. "It's a comedy depicting the couple's life-changing, spiritual existence after having become defined by the voice of a child.

"I will play the lead," she said humbly.

"It sounds interesting. I can't wait to see it. I am so proud of you."

They sat for a little while enjoying the view, talking about mutual acquaintances, when out of the blue,

"Jason, I am here to ask you to audition for the leading man."

"Ah-ha! The plot thickens," he said.

"We have such a wonderful working relationship and rapport with one another, not to mention the chemistry between us. Please, will you consider it?" Sunni pleaded. "Production will begin as soon as the leading man is cast. You are perfect for the part. What do you say?" she asked with a pouting lower lip.

Jason weighed each word, gazed into her doe blue eyes, and said, "This is unexpected. I must tell you I have settled in and comfortable at the farm for now. I love animals, and I love farm work. I have saved money, and I'm a pretty happy guy right now."

"Read the script, is all I ask," she begged.

"Yes! I will read the script, but I will not make any promises."

"Good! Now, will you join me for dinner?" she asked, "The menu is wonderful."

"I'd like to very much," he said.

Twenty-Six

When Shelby arrived at the farm, Chris greeted her with a warm smile as usual.

"Did you enjoy a good day?" he asked. His increased interest gave her joy, and Ms. Maude's gentle embrace confirmed the welcome Shelby always anticipated.

"Come, sit with me. Tell me about your week," Chris gestured, "Ms. Maude will bring us a glass of wine."

"Chris, I did enjoy a good week. I felt secure with all the precautions. She glanced around curiously before asking, "Where is Ms. Carlina? Will she join us?"

"Lana has one of her migraines and asked to dine in her room," Chris explained with a wrinkled brow and slight upward curve to his mouth.

Shelby suppressed her delight with a simple, "Oh!" She imagined Lana's migraine probably induced by her expected arrival.

After a quiet dinner, Shelby and Chris sat at a table in the garden. Shelby explained her conversation with Sam about expanding the newspaper, educating the townspeople on political issues, and interviewing people living in the hills.

"Shelby, your motive to interview people in the hills is admirable. My concern is these villagers developed independent rules over the years and have excluded law enforcement regulations. Visiting a primitive isolated society can lead to precarious endeavors for outsiders. If you are serious about interviewing these people, and knowing you as I am beginning to, I don't imagine you giving up until you see it through. Allow me to investigate first. I can, hopefully, locate a contact with insight on the area and reliable evaluation of its inhabitants.

"On yours and Sam's idea of expanding the paper, I approve. I'm especially interested in a series on understanding politics in general. I endorse the idea and offer any help or suggestions. Untapped potential in this community and outlying areas intrigues me as well," he said.

Shelby's interest in Chris escalated from him being a casual friend and protector to a mentor, a trusted confidant, an advisor, and maybe more. She smiled at him with respect and total admiration, but with his mind clouded over by their discussions, he stared into space, oblivious to her adoring gaze upon him.

Several days passed. Chris and Shelby began to spend more time together at the farm. They both enjoyed feeding the animals, grooming, and riding horses. Chris often referred to Shelby as 'the pretty farmhand.' Ms. Maude was pleased her employer displayed such happiness and contentment once again. She delighted in watching Chris's and Shelby's mutual interest in one another grow. She detected a courtship in the making, however subtle their interactions. Mr. Chris had always been laid back and sometimes secretive about his problems or desires. He showed little emotion when he dated briefly in Hollywood. The first time Ms. Maude found him absorbed totally in feeling was when he lost his mother. From then on, his endearing Ms. Maude became more to him than a housekeeper. She became his nurse, protector, and sounding board. However, Chris had not confided in her about his feelings toward Shelby.

Jason and Sunni renewed their friendship by dining together and riding horses at the farm. They quickly became inseparable, much to Lana's disgust. Since Jason had exhibited such talent in acting, she wished the notoriety as an actor for her son but remained meddlesome in his private life, affecting his past relationships. Not surprisingly, Sunni became an instant victim to Lana's prey.

Shelby listened to Jason laugh as he read numerous parts of the script Sunni had brought. He began talking to Chris and Shelby about some of the scenes. Shelby observed his interest in the film had escalated. After he read the script, he asked Chris for advice about auditioning for the movie. Chris, as he had done throughout Jason's younger years, quickly assured him of his capabilities of making decisions.

Shelby, still a guest at the farm, watched the drama with Jason's mother unfold. She remained constant support to Jason and Sunni while distancing away from Lana's never-ending snide remarks to Jason about the farm contributing as a career assassination, and his downfalls from dating 'common starlets'. Everyone waited for Jason's ultimate decision whether to accompany Sunni to Hollywood and audition. Chris, always diplomatic, attempted to keep everyone calm, especially Lana, who sometimes listened to him.

Twenty-Seven

Finally, the day for Sunni to return to Los Angeles arrived. Jason buckled under Sunni's persuasion and readied to accompany her to California. He would audition for the leading male role in the movie entitled ***Distinguished Voice.*** Lana hibernated at the farm when Chris and Shelby delivered the excited couple to the airport, which came as no surprise to anyone.

After Jason left, life at the farm returned to normalcy, or at least for Chris and Shelby, who continued their routines and regular methods of working. Ms. Carlina's role of entitlement required more attention from Ms. Maude to address her every whim.

Shelby prepared for eventful weeks ahead. The trial for the defendants who attempted her kidnapping and vandalized her property had scheduled. With new evidence of her near abduction, FBI agents found curious similarities in other cases, including the still-open cases of two missing women from the same area.

Because of the seriousness and ongoing threats to Shelby and others within the judicial system, Sheriff Tom ordered additional security around those involved. Attorneys, who had traveled from Richmond to assist, estimated a short trial after having studied the evidence.

Shelby's parents planned their stay at Jeremiah's Lodge while attending the trial. They inclined to worry less for their daughter's safety after having met Chris and

Ms. Maude while on a short trip to the farm, and of course, Ms. Carlina, who, Shelby's mother, claimed, "Is capable of scaring a barracuda."

Business resumed as usual at the newspaper office. Shelby and Sam worked toward expanding. They planned to intersperse a variety of topics, including political views by government figures and input relating associated press releases. Before the trial date, Sam asked Shelby how she would like to travel to Chicago. Sam realized ties with her former employer at the Chicago newspaper might give her an edge on contacting critical figures in a high-powered government.

"A good idea, Sam. I'll make some calls and see what I can line up. Political views from government figures I am acquainted with will be helpful.

During her visit to Chicago, Shelby engaged with people in government whom she had previously interviewed for the TRIBUE. Those available to meet with her expressed joy in seeing her again and their eagerness to help. All conveyed interest in her town and offered helpful suggestions on how to implement facts of government in a rural area. Her visit with the Lieutenant Governor proved most productive. He introduced political principles and gave opinions on how to obtain grant charters offering additional privileges to the townspeople. Shelby had gathered a wealth of information to relay to Sam. In the evening at the hotel, she measured all the contributing input, preprocessed together the intellectual and the emotional for her column, and visited with old friends before returning home. Once Shelby settled back in Poa, she wrote documentaries on systemized forms of government. She described, in laymen's terms, both civil and civic laws concerning citizens and government, and the importance of having an organized system of government. Shelby began by encouraging her readers to take an active interest in government issues. She introduced the basics and emphasized how politics are sometimes challenging to comprehend and how she was eager to learn along with the community. She outlined each article to entice her readers to hunger for more.

"Anyone can make a difference." she proclaimed.

"We will put this little town on the map," Sam told Shelby and planned for her to visit Washington and New York in the future.

Chris called Shelby aside after dinner Friday evening, "I am in contact with someone privy to connections with people in the hills," he told her. "He is willing to meet with us to discuss how to approach the Villagers. If you set up a meeting with Sam, we may reach a breakthrough."

"Chris, this is wonderful," she kissed his cheek. He reached for her hand as she started to turn, and as if on cue to upstage the star, Lana burst through the doorway.

"Well, sorry to interrupt," she snarled a rude apology as if passed over for a younger actress to replace her in a steamy love scene.

Shelby and Chris remained silent.

Later, Shelby phoned Sam and scheduled a meeting for them to meet with Chris and his contact. Upon listening to Shelby end her conversation, Lana followed her to the bottom of the staircase.

"How much longer should we expect you to stay as a guest in this house, Miss Evans?" Lana's low denounced voice did not shock or alarm Shelby's ability to resist such unsettling rudeness. She remained fixed in her position and nonchalantly answered in the most accentuated southern drawl she could muster, "Why Miss 'Cawhlina', I am like a family member by now, you all."

Lana glared at her in disbelief, disdainfully tossed her hair over one shoulder and trotted off with an "Oomph!" Ms. Maude's faint giggles from behind kitchen doors brought a smile to Shelby's lips. Thankfully, the weekend ended without further confrontations, but Shelby remained guarded for the next contemptuous remark.

Twenty-Eight

The following week passed quickly. The meeting with Shelby, Chris, Sam Shoney, and Chris's friend, Jake Beasley, took place at the newspaper office. Jake, a government official with an office in Richmond, held a job of importance to the State of Kentucky. He conducted periodic investigations on businesses, such as coal mines, making sure they were controlled according to regulations, offering significant help. He had become acquainted with coal miners living in the hill country and suggested he accompany them as a guide, when and if they prepared to go.

"I found the people I've talked to in the village are friendly and honest," Jake said, "They are living as their ancestors before them because they grew up knowing nothing else. The men are either miners or hunters and,"...he paused before continuing, "At one-time moonshine was a significant part of their existence. However, there are exaggerated tales rumored about people living in the hills of Appalachia. Other rumors are complete imaginary accounts from townspeople. Lack of knowledge is a temptation for sensationalism. No visible evidence supported felony crimes. Petty thieves, stealing from their neighbors, often face retaliation by victims, but are seldom resolved through violence.

"I agree with Ms. Evans; all children deserve a chance at education. We might be able to offer help and hope for people in the Appalachia area. Most of the inhabitants are approachable but no guarantee of the outcome of such an encounter."

Looking at Shelby, Beasley said, "Ms. Evans, you get a small group of people together you trust, and I will accompany the group as a guide!"

"Shelby, I'm not sure it's a good idea for you to go to the village under the circumstances of an assault against you," Chris said, protectively. "If you are sure bent on this, I suggest you put a group of able bodies together for the trip and position yourself at a command post for added protection. He explained the circumstances for his concern to Jake.

Later when alone, Chris over emphasized his concern to Shelby. "You are vulnerable to attack by those with threats against you. You are important to me, to all of us. I don't relish you being in harm's way."

Not quite a commitment, she guessed. Chris sounded like a worried parent by his concerns.

"Thanks, Chris, I appreciate your concern. I will work on getting a group together first and decide, based on the volunteers. I won't take any unnecessary chances. I promise."

Despite Chris's objections, Shelby intended to accompany the group to the hill country, as he expected she would. Monday morning at the paper, she and Sam discussed Beasley's input. They speculated on developing interest of the townspeople in the hill project but hadn't reached an agreement on an approach before the workweek ended on Friday.

Twenty-Nine

Shelby walked into the principal's office after dismissing her journalism class on Friday afternoon and brought Kate up to date on the meeting with Beasley.

"Kate, I need your input on this project."

"Shelby, how commendable of you to start such a project," Kate told her, "I am supportive and offer whatever I can to help. I am eager to help those families, especially the children. Now tell me what is going on at the farm?" Shelby had confided in her friend about Lana Carlina.

"How should I react to such rudeness? It isn't even her home. Chris would not approve of her comments, but I will not tell him what she said to me."

"Your rendition of Dolly Parton did just fine," Kate laughed.

"Does she view me as a threat? I don't have designs on her man if that's who he is."

"Why not attempt to make friends? Maybe invite her to your office, let her into your life a little. Pay her compliments and ask advice about wardrobe, etc. Inquire about her interests."

"I tried a few compliments but got nowhere. I view Ms. Lana Carlina as an unhappy woman without scruples or compassion. I'm sorry for her at times. To find out Jason is Lana's son is unbelievable to me. The primary interest Ms. Lana Carlina has is in Ms. Lana Carlina, and meddling in her son's business. Jason is such a delight, nothing like her. I miss having him close by. I hope to get through this period of my life and return to my cottage as soon as possible."

"What about Christopher Standish? Are the two of you getting close?"

"Chris is a good company, I can imagine falling for him, but don't dare entertain the option, especially with Carlina breathing down his back."

"Shelby, your face glows at the mention of his name. You've bonded with him in a way you are unaware, or are you unaware?"

"I might depend on him more than I should. Chris is someone I admire and respect. I can't read anything else into the relationship from him except compassion. I could have been mistaken for a creature from outer space when we first met."

"Are you happy spending time alone with him?"

"Yes! We frequently ride in the fields together and work together in the barns taking care of the animals. I detected, on occasion, maybe he would like to get close, but then something always happens, such as the time I expected he was going to kiss me, but then Lana suddenly appeared as if not treated with proper attention."

Kate raised an eyebrow, "There goes the gleam in your eye again, and you don't appear as a creature from outer space now."

Shelby ignored Kate's comment as if in deep concentration.

"We both enjoy quiet as well as conversation. Chris told me recently he is comfortable around me and can easily meditate when we are out riding. I don't know what he meant."

"He may be shy about making advances, displaying emotion. Maybe he hasn't dated often, or maybe he hasn't been interested until now."

"Kate, maybe you are also in the matchmaking profession," Shelby told her before leaving." They smiled at one another and waved goodbye.

At the cottage, a light on Shelby's phone blinked. She listened to a short message and returned a call to Jason.

"Shelby, I wanted to tell you first. The producers offered the part in Sunni's movie to me; I accepted. Also, I called to ask how you are and what is going on with the trial."

"Jason, I am so proud of you, in a movie or not. You are special. You will excel, no matter what you decide is right for your life. The trial is starting again after delays to gather evidence and keep the defendants peaceful without disruptions. I'm fine, besides spending time with the animals and riding with Chris, I write, teach at the school, and try to stay away from kidnappers."

She told him about her trip to Chicago and the newspaper expansion. She left out the part about planning to investigate the hill people, which she deemed too involved for a short conversation. After their goodbyes, Shelby placed the receiver on the cradle, thinking what joy he had brought into her life and the lives of others.

"He is so mature, way beyond his years," she said aloud.

After the deputy delivered Shelby to the farm, Chris, Ms. Maude, and Lana shared another call from Jason with his news. Shelby protectively omitted to tell them Jason relayed the story to her first on a previous phone call.

"Lana, you look especially nice today," said Shelby. Her attempt to tame grudging resentment and offer friendship affected a smirk of disregard from the actress.

Oh well, I tried! Shelby quietly credited a few points for effort.

Thirty

Before trial procedures on Monday morning, Shelby identified both Donnie Glasgow and Billy James Brown in a photographic line-up, "They are the two who terrorized me on the country road," she said.

To Shelby's surprise, businesses closed for the occasion. People in town gathered to capacity in the small courtroom. The judge was seated facing the jury and spectators before deputies leading the accused into the courtroom. Clean-shaven and outfitted as schoolboys, the defendants glared daggers at the prosecutor, and Shelby, sending chilling sensations throughout her body.

"Those two are the ones who terrorized and threatened me during the horrifying night on the dark country road," she said, pointing to Donnie Glasgow and Billy James Brown.

The other two, Willy and Otto, accused of participating in the home robbery, sat as codefendants. She did not recognize either. She testified as to the extent of the damages and stolen property.

The trial day came to an end. The four disgruntled defendants who attempted to kidnap Shelby, who vandalized her vehicle, invaded her home practically destroying her possessions, and who stole expensive equipment were hurried away in shackles, escorted by their jailers. Chris Standish and Sam Shoney realized, by the demeanor of the defendants and their supporters, retaliation remained a potential threat from behind bars.

"This is far from over," the two men sorrowfully predicted.

The next day Shelby walked out to meet two deputies as her escorts, instead of one. Chris explained later in the evening.

"Shelby, the Sheriff heightened your security again in light of the circumstances. None of us want to take chances of putting you in harm's way."

Shelby stared at him, void of expression, and forced a smile. Her lips began to pulsate a quiver when she attempted to speak. The truth, Shelby was embarrassed. She blamed herself for becoming a burden to everyone who had become involved with protecting her.

"I am so sorry to put you and everyone else through this," she apologized.

"Shelby, dear, keep in mind, this is not your doing. You are an unwilling player in a vile and loathsome act by criminals. Security is precautionary reasoning. Our job is to keep you safe and to ensure justice. He hugged her with more compassion than before and kissed a tear upon her cheek, wiling away all fears and anxiety. The warmth of his breath and safety net of his arms stirred her emotions into a frenzied state between desired passion and a relaxed feeling under a shield of protection. For a moment, she sank into contemplation until he spoke.

"What happened to you has possibly led to taking criminals off the street and saving other victims. Now, let's join the others, eat dinner, and give thanks for your safety and Maude's good dinner."

Shelby worked at her computer all day Saturday, pausing long enough to devour lunch treats Ms. Maude prepared.

"Ms. Maude is like having another mother looking out for me," she told her Mom. "She not only takes special care to serve proper nutrients to everyone at the farm but gives respectful consideration to every individual. Everyone is special to her. Somehow, she manages a polite word while attending to Ms. Carlina's every whim."

Monday, they attended another trial day, and Tuesday, another. For Shelby, the hours and days moved slowly. Fingerprints collected at Shelby's home and in her vehicle proved to authorities, beyond a doubt, the presence of all four defendants in her home. The prosecutor presented all four defendants as capable of violent crimes, but Donnie Glasgow and Billy James Brown faced additional serious charges: attempted kidnapping, terroristic threatening, etc. Before the Judge waited to hear their pleas, they screamed loud protests and demonstrated fits of anger, stomping, and waving their arms. All four defendants began to feed on one another, cursing, damning the police, and threatening to sue the city. The unyielding judge faced the four defendants with a stern commination, confirming he would tolerate no-nonsense in his courtroom. He pounded his gavel on the oversized desk and motioned for deputies to lead all four prisoners away. They shuffled along, their shackles dragging clanking chains across the floor.

The following trial day, Willie and Otto remained stoic while the conduct of Glasgow and Brown escalated to another fiasco as in the previous day. The public defender failed to calm either prisoner. The courtroom housed another so-called circus event. The defendants jumped up and down, stormed toward the judge, screamed, pointed at the prosecutor, and Shelby, cursing and calling names. Terrified, Shelby relived their threats from the lonely road. Horrified onlookers gasped.

Judge Hiram Morley pounded his gavel, and deputies seized all four of the defendants and led them away while the two of them shouted slurs and obscenities.

"Court proceedings will adjourn. Keeping the defendants incarcerated for a while might calm them enough for better conduct in the courtroom," Judge Morley declared to the courtroom full of spectators. "These proceedings are canceled for six weeks. Please clear the courtroom."

Thirty-One

Considering the interim, Sam approached Shelby to plan a trip to visit Washington for interviews, as she and Sam had discussed. She agreed, and Sam made calls to a few political friends.

"The people I've suggested for you to contact are friendly and easy to approach, unlike some of the other members of the Senate," Sam told her, "their input can be of tremendous value to our documentaries. I inquired as to their availability, and all are willing to meet with you if you call for an appointment."

Shelby's intuition told her Chris instigated the decision to send her out of town for her safety, and Sam implemented the plan. How does Chris manage so much influence? Who exactly is Christopher Standish? She wondered.

The following Sunday afternoon, Shelby checked into the Washington Plaza Hotel in Washington DC at Ten North West Thomas Circle. She unpacked and at once began to prepare for the next few days. Her first scheduled interviews for the following day included brief discussions with a senator from Indiana, one from Ohio, and a Kentucky State Representative. All went exceptionally well. She listened intently, took notes, and discussed needed improvements in her county. She planned interviews for the next day, including one with the secretary of a Kentucky State Senator in the Senator's absence.

After dinner, with time on her hands, Shelby walked through the hotel lobby and admired its unique charm. The nine-floor, 340 room, u-shaped high-rise hotel, constructed in 1962, attracted politicians and business executives because of its amenities and downtown location.

While tucked away in her hotel room the second night, Shelby called her editor, "Everything is going well," she reported to Sam Shoney. The two chatted about her trip, the hotel amenities, and the personalities of those with whom she had met. Sam praised her for a good job, and they said their goodbyes.

Later, curious, and with time on her hands, Shelby began a personal internet search. She uncovered a magazine article and short biography on Lana Carlina, that read in part: ***A representative of PLAYBOY magazine approached Lana Carlina, a bright-eyed beauty whose picture as a winning beauty pageant contestant appeared in the TRIBUNE. When discovering she was too young at seventeen to appear in PLAYBOY, an agent pursued her for the possibility of movie roles.***

However, Shelby found in a follow-up story, Carlina had become older, shy of her thirtieth birthday before her debut in a movie caught the eye of a young director. The article described how the young, up and coming director, Christopher Stone discovered Carlina's talent and cast her in a film called ***Embrace,*** written by the author, Trace Sutherland. Shelby continued to read headlines in the tabloids claiming instant stardom for Carlina, dubbing her the newest darling of the big screen, crediting her with prominence. The same article claimed Stone received a career boost and acclaim for promoting her career.

"I remember the movie as a tale of infidelity and mistrust involving a young married couple who lived in an established community of older professionals," Shelby said aloud, "I didn't make the connection.

Shelby, absorbed in the findings, became increasingly interested in the mysterious woman who viewed her as a challenge. Suddenly, a loud knock on her hotel room door startled her. The fact the time was after 9:00 pm was suspicious.

"Yes, who's there?" she asked, timidly.

"Front desk, ma'am! Delivery."

Shelby refused to open the door. "I am not expecting anything. Are you sure you are in the right room?"

"Are you Ms. Evans?"

The past shattering events had led to her becoming paranoid, but she opened the door cautiously, keeping the chain locked. She recognized the uniform of a hotel employee who held a bouquet. She unlocked the chain, took the flowers, thanked him, and quickly closed the door. Inside her room, she examined the flowers, a scant bunch of white lilies without a card, and wrapped in newspaper. Her imagination spun.

"This is suspicious," she said aloud and called her parents. They denied sending the flowers. She called Sam Shoney, who immediately called Standish. No one within her circle of friends or relatives had sent the flowers.

"No one knows I am here except you, Sam and my parents, she told Chris.

"Shelby, I will follow up on this. Quickly place the flowers in the hall for the maid. Stay in the room. Don't open the door for anyone. Keep the latch and chain bolted," he cautioned. "Don't be frightened."

"I'm a little frightened, but I don't understand how anyone associated with the boys on trial might have found me."

"What about contacts you made during the day?" he asked.

No one asked where I was staying, and I didn't offer. These flowers are wrapped in newspaper as if plucked out of someone's yard," she said.

"I see," he said. "I don't anticipate a connection to those on trial, but we won't take unnecessary chances. Keep your chin up. I will contact the hotel manager. Someone may have recognized a truck from the florist or remember the delivery person," he spoke with a persuasive voice, however unconvincing to Shelby or himself.

Shelby decided not to fret about the flowers and followed her internet search and the life of Lana Carlina while waiting for Chris's call.

"After all, this is public knowledge," she mumbled, a little guilty about penetrating the world of Lana Carlina and Christopher Standish. Why am I doing this? Is my interest in Chris beyond a casual sense of inquisitiveness as a reporter?"

Another search led Shelby to Carlina's elaborate Hollywood wedding to Derrick Vance, her leading man in ***Embrace.*** Tabloids, quick to ascertain the wedding lasted longer than the marriage, sensationalized the couple's breakup, and magnetized the considerable value of their careers.

Shelby read a statement by Carlina to the effect, her husband, in realization, did not portray upstanding characters he played in movies. In real life, he was no more than a drunken misfit and an all-around ladies' man.

Oh! Derrick Vance is Jason's father, Shelby assumed and continued reading.

Sought by agents, especially by Jasper Clinton, known for stepping away from the norm or out of the box as described, Carlina

is known for having a fiery personality. She has a history of boisterous and sometimes crude on and off the set behavior. Her ability to minimize works of rival stars is nothing short of unprofessional and borders cruelty, threatening legal actions. Carlina has become dubbed, 'The Difficult Diva'.

Shelby read where Carlina and Stone remained friends, and how Stone became a role model and mentored her young son, Jason. A quote from a notorious Hollywood reporter who interviewed a friend of Stone's stated, ***Friend, Christopher Stone passes off Carlina's attitude and irrational behavior as a result of pain she suffered at the hands of the media, recounting her troubles and failed marriage. Stone further declared..." Lana's outbursts are a cover for the hurt she suffered. She reacts to avoid showing a vulnerable side."***

Shelby read in a celebrity news article where Stone had left Hollywood suddenly, explaining he had scheduled time off to take a break. His whereabouts remained confidential to the public.

Shelby sat in silence. She concluded Christopher Standish and Christopher Stone were the same. He probably played an essential role in Jason's life, maybe even raising him. She surmised. I have a better understanding of Lana. Perhaps I should try harder to befriend her.

Shelby closed her computer and waited for Chris's call when suddenly, she remembered the flowers and opened the door quietly to place them into the hallway.

Thirty-Two

Chris called Shelby's room. No answer. He called again and again. When she failed to answer, a sudden chill entered his body. He instructed the hotel manager to go in with a key if no one answered the door.

After checking the room, the hotel manager called security and reported back to Chris, "The place is in disarray as if a struggle occurred. Glass from a shattered wall mirror covers the floor. An empty purse is on the dresser, and a pair of shoes scattered as if lost in a scuffle. Broken stems and pedals of Lilies sprinkle the floor of the room, some strewn into the hallway. Security is trying to locate Miss Evans. We notified the police.

"A desk clerk reported he spoke to someone attempting to take flowers to Ms. Evans' room. He described the man as a street person and took the flowers from him, not allowing him the room number or access to the elevator. Our security officer said it appeared to him as if she opened the door to place the flowers in the hall when someone surprised her and violently threw her back into the room."

Shelby Evans had disappeared!

A dulling bite of panic entered Chris's body. He struggled with the realization of Shelby's kidnapping kidnapped.

Chief Jeffries jumped into action and contacted the Washington police, "One of our citizens, a key witness in a robbery and attempted abduction is in your city. She is in grave danger," the Chief's message brought forth immediate action from law enforcement and the FBI.

"I shouldn't have told her to place the flowers in the hall," Chris confessed to Tom Jeffries, "She would've been safer here under the protection of our local law enforcement and at the farm."

The FBI, once again, called upon to investigate a kidnapping relating to the town of Poa, arrived within minutes. Shelby, without a doubt, had become a victim of abduction. The hotel immediately came under total lockdown while Washington law enforcement posted a sentry at every entrance. Neither employees nor guests could leave or enter the building without permission.

Shelby's parents gasped in terror. Chris told them he vowed to use everything within his power to bring her to safety.

"I am confident we'll find her," he told them, "time is on our side."

Law enforcement invaded every corner of the building, including all 340 sleeping rooms. They questioned guests and employees; Agents searched the basement, which housed laundry facilities and storage. They searched stairwells and elevators. Hours passed before two hotel guests remembered seeing hooded figures running through the rear parking lot. Did this mean someone forced Shelby away from the property?

Standish summoned Private Detective Cravens, who was in town on leave from his Italy assignment. He arrived within minutes and stationed near a command center set up by the FBI inside the hotel lobby. Cravens considered everyone a potential suspect and began scrutinizing every hotel guest and employee. He found a guest who remembered seeing two men drag a third person appearing drunk toward the elevator. Cravens instantly returned to the elevator surveillance cameras. He viewed two people dressed in black and wearing hoods. They left the elevator on Shelby's floor. The two with their faces obscured by hoods dragged the third person, barefoot, toward the elevator. An FBI agent reviewed the video with Cravens. They agreed the person pulled along was likely the missing Shelby. Later, another video showed three people scurrying down the hall toward a rear entrance. Their characteristics were the same, but the clothing on two of them differed slightly. The third person was younger. Cravens and an FBI agent determined the individuals with hoods changed shirts while on the elevator to avoid suspicion.

As hope diminished for Shelby to have remained in the building, agents widened their search to other areas for two or three individuals traveling together to Appalachia. Within a short length of time, telephone wires began burning with inquiries and instructions. Police set up roadblocks, searched cars, and questioned drivers, including ones who were least suspicious. Agents at airport ticket counters were placed on alert.

Thirty-Three

Hours passed; Cravens contacted Standish with discouraging news.

"Everything is being done efficiently, in a steadfast manner. I can't understand what we are missing. I am going to double-check the hotel and will get back to you."

"Thanks, Cravens, I depend on you. This girl is important to me personally," he spoke as if he had instantly realized a bond of affection he held for her.

Chris turned to the flashing light on his phone and returned a missed call.

"Jason, you, Shelby's parents, and I can better help by staying where we are and wait for news from the FBI or Cravens. We need not challenge them by interruptions. I will call the moment of an update."

"Thanks, Chris. I count on you, always." Jason's voice remained solemn as they said their goodbyes.

Cravens and one of the local law enforcement officers retraced steps through the building for a closer look. On the ground floor stairwell leading to the basement and laundry facility, the officer shouted to Cravens.

"OVER HERE! TAKE A LOOK!" He held out strands of blond hair matching Shelby's, as seen in the photograph provided to officers. "I found this clinging to the railing, but we searched the laundry and storage rooms."

"This is an important clue," said Cravens, "If they brought her down here, they brought her to leave her here. We are going to tear this place apart, starting with the industrial washers and dryers."

The officer agreed and brought searchlights. He began slinging doors from dryers and washers, but no trace of the missing young woman.

"OVER HERE, "Cravens cried out with urgency," GET THE PARAMEDICS QUICKLY," he yelled to the policeman, "SHE'S HERE,"

Cravens' first glimpse of Shelby's lifeless body lying in a fetal position inside an oversized dryer in a remote area caused him tremendous alarm. He quickly examined her and thankfully found a pulse. Paramedics rushed inside from the street level outside the hotel.

"SHE'S ALIVE," Cravens shouted in desperation, "HURRY!" he demanded.

Medical corpsmen found Shelby's pulse seriously weak. They administered oxygen and gently examined her but cautioned everyone, "Until she is examined extensively by x-ray equipment and hospital personnel, her condition cannot be determined."

Upon hearing news from Cravens, Chris alerted Shelby's family, along with Jason and Ms. Maude. He told them she had been found alive and on the way to the hospital, nothing more. Everyone prayed and defenselessly waited.

Chris confessed to Ms. Maude, "I take responsibility for Shelby going to Washington. If I hadn't been so intent on reasoning, she would be safer away from here; this wouldn't have happened."

"There you go, Mr. Chris, again taking the blame for things out of your control."

Ms. Maude often sought to console him when she detected his sadness.

"This young woman has endured too much for me not to use everything I can to help her. I can't lose her, too. I'm going to Washington."

By his comment and the despair in his eyes, Ms. Maude sensed Chris had developed a more personal interest in Shelby than even he had realized. She merely hugged him, and at his request, notified the airport to contact the pilot and ready his plane.

"I will call you, dear Ms. Maude," he said.

A teary-eyed Maude clasped her hands in despair and stared at the door when he left. She turned toward the heavens and prayed aloud.

Chris's Cessna Citation reached Washington within a few hours of Shelby's arrival at the hospital.

"Cravens, thank you so much for picking me up. What else can you tell me? Is she alive? Did the dryer rotate? Did she suffer burns? Chris's questions spilled out while he braced for answers.

"Yes, Standish, she is alive as of ten minutes ago, and no indications of severe burns. Evidence indicated the dryer rotated; how many times, not determined. Her arms or legs probably slammed against the inside of the machine, causing the door to unlatch and stop the rotation, saving her life. You can expect her to have fractures. The doctor has, so far, confirmed a concussion."

News reporters picked up Shelby's story as someone they considered one of their fellow peers. Media members flooded the hospital with questions. Shelby's home county became a target for personal details.

The DAILY RECORD gave an account of Shelby's kidnapping, torture, and hospitalization. The Washington Post, USA Today, and the Tabloids blew Chris's cover when someone recognized him at the hospital. Christopher Stone's celebrity status in Hollywood and the fact gossip columnists often described him as one of Hollywood's most eligible bachelors, made him newsworthy. After a reporter revealed the identity of Christopher Stone, alias Standish, it didn't take long for the media to provide notoriety to one little country county in Kentucky.

Thirty-Four

Media personnel set up shop in the middle of the Appalachian Plateau. Crews embellished the old country road and the countryside surrounding the Standish farmhouse much as a movie set. Reporters scrambled for a juicy story of why Stone had left Hollywood to live in exile under a false name and in a remote area. They wanted to know his relationship with a fellow reporter and the story behind her abduction. They set up cameras and production equipment as close to the Standish farm as possible, inviting curious townspeople to meander about attempting to obtain information enough to embellish stories to their neighbors. Sheriff Jeffries arranged for added security around the farm.

Law enforcement conclusively established order in the county but was ill-equipped to prevent the media intrusion. Unemployed coal miners attempted to apply for employment or become cast in films. Utter confusion consumed the town, but shop owners whose businesses thrived, welcomed the intruders.

Ms. Maude sought comfort in the seclusion of her private quarters, while Lana packed to return to California. She conspicuously drove her rental car to the local airport with paparazzi in tow. She ignored them with her haughty glances and scornful words but lavished the attention.

At the Washington hospital, Shelby remained in a medically induced coma.

"All we can do is wait and pray," said the doctor. "The extent of her injuries include a skull fracture, swelling in the brain, a fractured arm and leg, and extensive bruising. The fact there were no burns decided the dryer made few rotations. She has suffered one hard blow to her head. A prognostic predictive will evaluate after she awakens."

Chris, along with Shelby's parents, remained at her side as often as allowed. Chris introduced himself to the hospital staff as a family member, which permitted him into the intensive care unit. When Shelby stabilized, the Doctor had her moved into a private room. Chris spared no expense by providing around the clock private nurses.

Satisfied with the Doctor's thumbs up on Shelby's condition, and the fact the media frenzy escalated to the hospital attempting to corner him, Chris prepared to leave for Kentucky after he spoke to reporters as a family spokesperson. He asked them to please give Ms. Evans and her family the privacy needed for her recovery.

A tearful Ms. Maude greeted Chris when he arrived home to face a slew of paparazzi. He asked media personnel to respect his privacy, and he would reciprocate by giving each an interview. The next day he honored his promise and answered questions to their satisfaction, effectively deciding most to leave.

In discovering what family members of the defendants went missing the time of Shelby's abduction, the FBI located a ticket agent at the Poa terminal office who identified Abel and Hank Glasgow as the two who claimed to want to purchase tickets to travel on the same flight as their sister. They gave Shelby's name as their sister and left without buying a ticket.

When apprehended on their way toward Kentucky, they claimed to be returning from a fishing trip. However, with no fishing equipment in their possession, and multiple reasons to suspect them, law enforcement took them into custody and placed them high on their list of suspects. Still, it wouldn't be until enough evidence surfaced for arrests to occur. At the time of the brothers' arrest, Jeb Clayton had disappeared. Since he was under suspicion of kidnapping and attempted murder the same as the other two, a warrant for his arrest was issued as well.

Getting rid of a lot of the riffraff elated the town members. "A total of six, now in jail, and another sought," one of the prosecutor's remarked, "This is a grand opportunity for a public defender looking for work."

"We questioned Mildred, the younger sister of Jeb Clayton, after she confided in her teacher at school. She and her mother feared for Jeb's safety," the Sheriff told Christopher Standish, or Stone, now that his secret is out.

The youngster cried to the principal, "My brother's friends did bad things and said they would shut Jeb up before they went to jail, and now Jeb is missing."

The child is afraid Jeb is in danger. She's frightened for her brother's safety. We've reason to expect he is in danger as well and making use of all our resources to locate him."

After Sheriff Jeffries interviewed teachers and found Jeb was a good student who had never been in trouble and confirmed by Mrs. Clayton, the search for Jeb heightened. Available deputies and several volunteers searched every farm, vacant building, and unattended pasture. After hours of searching, deputies came upon a dilapidated shed on an abandoned farm where they found Jeb bound and tied to an old tie beam. His condition was grave. He suffered from knife wounds, fractures, severe bruising, and dehydration. Because of his critical condition and lack of response, officers called for air transportation and sent him by helicopter to Richmond to a hospital with a trauma unit.

Thirty-Five

Sunday morning, after Shelby lay in a coma for two weeks, doctors told her mother, "Shelby is likely to awaken at any time." John and Janet Evans remained at their daughter's bedside as often as possible, worried about permanent effects from her injuries.

"Will she recover? What about her memory or brain damage? Will she recognize us?" Janet plagued the doctors with questions.

Janet sat in the hospital room, agonized, listening to faint sounds of murmurs rasping from Shelby's throat. All at once, her daughter's eyelashes fluttered. Her fingers began to move slightly and started to moan in short breaths. Janet called for the nurse.

"Shelby, are you in pain? Can you hear me?" The nurse calmly asked questions.

The doctor on call was summoned and checked her reflexes, "She seems ok where paralysis is concerned. Talk to her, he said to Janet, "she may recognize your voice."

"Shelby, can you hear me? It's Mom. Please open your eyes. Talk to me. Do you hurt anywhere?" Shelby remained silent with her eyes closed. Her arms went limp.

"What is happening?" Janet whimpered, anxiously waiting for the doctor to speak.

"Mrs. Evans, I don't have an answer at this point. The neurologist who is more experienced in this type of injury is on the way here.

Once the doctor left Shelby's room, her Mom sat staring at her daughter, praying for any type of movement, a reflex, anything at all.

Hours passed. Janet quietly sobbed at her daughter's bedside when,

"Mom, what is wrong?" Shelby uttered.

Amazingly, Shelby had awakened and attempted to sit up.

"Oh, Shelby! "Janet shouted her daughter's name.

"What is going on? Why are you crying?" Shelby murmured.

The neurologist had arrived and hurried into Shelby's room after hearing the commotion. Janet braced against the door, motionless while the doctor rushed to examine his patient. The two of them, along with the private nurse, began talking in a nucleus of excitement, everyone directed questions to the patient.

Shelby awkwardly struggled to sit. She faced them, focused on the doctor, and demanded to know what made her Mom cry, and why she was in bed.

"We will explain everything to you, Shelby," said the doctor. Shelby's voice signaled weak and throaty sounds, but by all accounts, she was alert. The neurologist asked Shelby's mother to wait outside the room. He and the nurse remained in Shelby's hospital room several minutes before he gave Janet an update on her condition.

"Mrs. Evans, your daughter, has suffered a severe physical and emotional shock. I can only explain a miracle beyond what we understand about the laws of nature saved her life from such a deplorable crime. Her vitals are good," he said with conviction. "Her short-term memory is amiss but will improve with time. I told her what happened to her. With effort and concentration, she remembered the hotel, and she remembered opening the door from inside her room, but she doesn't remember the assault. When a person experiences trauma such as Shelby, both mental and physical, the brain enables them to experience less pain. It is one of God's perks. I am happy to tell you I expect a full recovery over time.

"I will arrange for her to remain in the hospital a while longer, depending on her progress, of course. It will give time for her bruising and fractures on her feet and leg to begin to heal.

"If she remains as she is now and continues to improve, she will move to a private room tomorrow. Once she is released, she will need care until the fractures in her feet heal," said the doctor.

"Thank you, Doctor, we are so grateful," Janet Evans' joyful tears fell from her cheeks as she hugged the doctor. Her father and I will care for her until she can live alone."

Janet went directly to the phone and called her husband first and then Chris, who contacted a relieved Jason in California. Shelby's friends in Chicago, along with everyone in her Kentucky County, celebrated the joyful news.

Shelby's condition upgraded after two weeks. The day before her discharge, the nurse announced the arrival of visitors. She raised her head and smiled at the happy face of Ms. Maude, flanked by a grinning Chris, who carried a dozen red roses to add to the flowers from well-wishers and to ones he previously sent. With emotions easily affected by their visit, and her weakened condition, Shelby struggled to hide tears. The visitors prepared to leave after a short time, not wanting her to use all her strength before leaving the hospital the next day.

"When you get settled at your parents, I will call and give you an update of what is happening at home," Chris told her. He gently kissed her cheek and bade her farewell.

The next morning before leaving the hospital, Shelby thoughtfully donated flowers that had consumed her room to the children's ward, except for the red roses she insisted on taking with her. Chris and Ms. Maude accompanied her to the airport. Chris had provided a private hospital jet to transport Shelby, her mother, and a nurse to Indiana.

"So much attention," she said. "I don't deserve all this."

Chris smiled and kissed her cheek.

Thirty-Six

Work at the RECORD was still not back to normal, but Sam refused to hire anyone to take his assistant's place. His wife, Betty, volunteered to help by answering phones while her husband worked on gathering news to report. He kept readers abreast of Shelby's recovery, and updated incarcerations of her accused offenders.

Kate stayed in touch with Shelby by computer and by phone. She enlightened her on matters concerning the 'hill people' and progress in her journalism class.

"Sam Shoney is enjoying your journalism class as an interim teacher. You made a positive impact on him, the children, the school, and to a lot of us," she said.

"A lot of the children sent cards and drawings to me," Shelby said.

"The children are continuing to make drawings for you," Kate told her.

"I am so grateful to you, Sam, and everyone. Thank you so much, Kate. You are a good friend.

"I'm writing articles again and developing more kinetic energy," she told her friend, "I'm walking better and tried riding my old nag, Duffy. She doesn't compare to Chris's horses, but she is a good friend. I also began painting again, and my mom's friend at the local art gallery has asked me to exhibit some of my work, which I plan to do after completion.

"That's wonderful. I love what I've seen of your paintings. Hurry and get well. We miss you."

"Thanks, I will stay in touch."

In the afternoon, after a call from Chris, Shelby confided in her mother, "I miss riding horses at Chris's farm; I miss everyone I have gotten to know in the community."

"Shelby, I'm not sure you miss the horses as much as you miss Chris," her mother said lovingly."

"Yes, I miss Chris, Ms. Maude, Jason, and the animals. I don't miss Lana." They both snickered.

"I understand she moved back to California," her mother said.

"Yes, the notoriety at the farm became hectic for her. She went to Hollywood and a peaceful environment," they both laughed.

"My regret is, because of me, Chris's identity became known to the media, and his seclusion compromised. They're all hungry for a juicy story."

"The same as you would be," Janet said. "Does Chris say what his plans are?"

"The filming industry is hounding him to produce and direct now that he has

publicly surfaced. He said he volunteered to help with Jason's film as a temporary assignment. He didn't elaborate. He plans to visit family in Italy to conduct some personal business. He didn't say what kind of business. Chris and Jason stay busy. I don't talk to either of them as often."

"Shelby, you made an impact on Jason as well as Chris and Ms. Maude. Jason called me several times before you left the hospital," Janet told her daughter.

After several weeks of recovery, Shelby returned to Kentucky and her job at the RECORD. She effortlessly worked at school teaching journalism and worked on a plan to visit the hill country. On her off days, Shelby visited Ms. Maude at the farm at Chris's request. He suggested she ride horses as part of her therapy. Shelby conjectured hers, and Chris's relationship had developed beyond a casual friendship, and waited anxiously for him to return.

Sheriff Jeffries kept Shelby abreast of the investigation. He told her, " Recent evidence against the desperadoes suspected of your kidnapping, has surfaced. Distinguishing characteristics related to crimes against you are significantly like the cases of the two women who went missing in this area some time ago. Until now, those cases began to die out without further evidence. What happened to you has given support to facts instrumental in solving those cases. If anything significant comes to mind in your abduction, please give me a call. Anything you might add may help with the other two cases as well. I believe we'll find a connection."

"Thank you, Sheriff; I will let you know if I can remember anything."

In the afternoon, Shelby received another call from the Sheriff's office, "Ms. Evans, Sheriff Tom asked me to call you," the deputy said. "Thankfully, we found young Jeb in time. He is in the hospital in Richmond."

"Oh! My goodness. What happened?"

"The bad guys planned his demise as well. They left him beaten and starving, tied up in an old shed. It was a scheme for them to escape blame. Jeb can't speak. With his mouth swollen and missing some teeth," he's receiving medical attention and is under police protection. The FBI is waiting to question him. His survival is under wraps at this point. We don't want the Glasgow brothers to have a heads up. Deputies will stay close by you, but please stay alert to your surroundings."

"I will. Thank you."

The trial for the four in jail in Poa resumed the next day and lasted two weeks. The defendants continued to claim the police framed them but buttoned-down after their long jail term the judge ordered. Shelby identified the two who terrorized her. Her description of how they attempted her abduction on a lonely country road causing her to sleep among howling critters until daylight horrified the jury and on-lookers. Evidence collected against them convicted Donnie Glasgow and Billy James Brown of attempted kidnapping and burglary and sentenced them to a maximum-security inside a Florida prison for twenty years. They would not receive a parole hearing for twelve years. The other two, Willie and Otto, convicted of burglary and destruction of property, received a lighter sentence and were sent to a prison near Lexington, Kentucky.

The two brothers, uncles of Glasgow, awaited trial in Washington for the assault, kidnapping, and attempted murder of Shelby. The third defendant, Jeb Clayton, recuperated at an unknown location under temporary witness protection.

Thirty-Seven

Once Jeb recovered enough to travel, the trial in Washington scheduled. Although Shelby's memory loss prevented her from visibly identifying her abductors at the hotel in Washington, Assistant District Attorney, Nigel Adams, summoned her as a critical witness. This time, Shelby, along with law enforcement, planned extra precautions. She and her mother enjoyed VIP treatment at the hotel where her abduction had taken place. A Washington policeman who stationed outside their hotel room gave them added security, not only as a precautionary measure but a goodwill effort by local authorities and support from hotel management.

National media, along with Shelby's friends, adherent supporters, and co-workers with whom she worked previously, created a hullaballoo among themselves and a demand for justice. Chris's celebrity status and Shelby's journalism assignment in Washington involving high-profile politicians created a media frenzy of notoriety overnight.

Shelby gave a riveting testimony with Judge H. Quincy Cahill presiding. She described what she remembered when she opened her hotel room door but was unable to identify the assailants.

"I remember seeing, briefly, two figures with hoods. I experienced an elevated sensation as if flying backward. I remember waking up and feeling sick to my stomach. My head hurt unbearably. Afterward, everything went black. I can't remember anything else until I awakened in the hospital," her voice quivered as if reliving a shocking experience of pain. Shelby's testimony and Adams' account of her having been knocked unconscious, dragged to the basement, and thrown into a large industrial dryer, and left to die, visibly disturbed the court assembly and visitors. Her former boyfriend, Tony, and co-workers from Chicago were stunned.

When escorted to her seat, Shelby's wandering eyes danced around the courtroom. She nodded her appreciation toward her former co-workers when she unexpectedly caught a rapturous gaze from none other than Christopher Stone, alias Standish. She discreetly smiled at him. Her emotions kindled a pang of excitement. The two had been apart since she left the hospital weeks before.

The trial continued with testimony by the Glasgow brothers. They rambled on in nonsensical, jabberwocky distortion, unworthy of belief. They pointed an accusing finger at Jeb Clayton and said he ran off to Mexico because he was guilty. When all failed, each attempted to blame the other and ridiculed themselves. They continually changed stories.

The conspicuous absence of friends and family members of the Glasgow brothers characterized their lack of connection to family supporters. After so much drama from the accused, Judge Cahill closed proceedings until the next day.

"Finally, I can catch up with Chris," Shelby said to her mother, when from out of the crowd, Tony, her former boyfriend, rushed to her side and embraced her. Her reporter friends from Chicago, gathered in an extended circle to give Shelby support before they scurried off to relay their embellished reports. It became impossible for her to elude them. Shelby agreed for Tony to pick her and her mother up for dinner in the evening only to get him to leave. So taut with emotions, Shelby rushed to locate Chris. She searched everywhere until the courthouse began to empty of all spectators and personnel. And, at the hotel, a message left by Chris explained a plane waited to take him to California. His schedule obligated him to meet a deadline. The note pledged his pride in her, and how wonderful she looked, signed, ***Affectionately, Chris.***

Janet understood clearly that her daughter's interest in Chris meant more to Shelby than she was willing to admit.

"He has commitments in Hollywood, Shelby, from what you told me," Janet said to her daughter, "I'm sure he will contact you soon."

Shelby regarded her mother's words of wisdom with care. She considered Chris's sudden departure as a pledge of a previous commitment and readied to keep their date with Tony. She had always enjoyed Tony's compromising personality and creative sense of humor. However, her affection for him remained as a kindred nature. When Shelby realized, through his indirect suggestion of marriage during the time they dated, he might be leading to a proposal, she told him they should start seeing other people. Tony responded by entering a brief seclusion away from all his friends and plunged into his work.

Why has he surfaced after all this time? She questioned. Is he hoping this is an opportunity for him to resume our dating relationship? I can't mislead him."

Fortunately, the evening ended pleasantly without innuendoes of personal relationships. After dinner, Tony escorted Shelby and her mother to their hotel, where he readied to leave them. He told them of his plan to return to Chicago the next morning and offered himself at their disposal in the future. His mannerisms confirmed to Shelby; he intended to rekindle their friendship and not a romantic relationship.

Thirty-Eight

When Jeb Clayton, recovering from his beatings, entered the courtroom in a wheelchair, gasps of surprise sent wild echoes from the walls. Abel and Hank Glasgow turned pale in disbelief. They glared at each other and Jeb.

Abel whispered to Hank, "Why aint he daid?"

Jeb's tearful mother and his sister, Mildred, sat submissively in support of him. When Jeb began to give his testimony, he stumbled through a confession. His body shook wretchedly, giving a tearful account of what happened after a night of partying.

"Hank Glasgow held my arms around behind me while Abel Glasgow poured liquor down my throat. They told me if I didn't go with them, I would be sorry. I was scared not to go," he said. "They threatened to hurt my sister if I wouldn't go with them," he whimpered.

"They took that girl to the basement and told me they just tied her up," he said, pointing to Shelby, "I didn't believe them. I was scared for her. They wouldn't take me back to show me. When the police started lookin for us, they beat me up and put me in a ole shed and said they would come back for me later, and then they laughed. I'm sorry I went with them, they shouldn't a done what they did. They are just mean," he sobbed.

"Who beat you?" Asked Adams.

"Them Glasgow's, Hank and Abel," he said, pointing to the other two defendants.

The Glasgow brothers yelled in protest. They shook their arms in rage and shouted obscenities at Jeb, blaming him for Shelby's kidnapping. The public defender, Marvin Jacobs, tried to quiet them, but they shoved him away. Judge Cahill intervened and had the two prisoners removed before calmly allowing Jeb to finish his testimony. Jeb's willingness to accept punishment and sobs of regret blanketed a hushed silence throughout the courtroom.

The trial became intense during the following days. Ms. Maude, who surprised Shelby and Janet by a visit, sat alongside them in the courtroom.

Outbursts by Hank and Abel Glasgow demanded Jeb lied about them. Attorney Jacobs quieted them as well as possible, and in support of his commitment to defend them, professed the evidence against them was insufficient to prove beyond a reasonable doubt. The outbursts prompted several questions to both attorneys by jury members. Consequently, answers benefitted the prosecution. The Glasgow brothers absurdly pledged their innocence, but the evidence told otherwise. Testimony from young Jeb Clayton vastly overpowered baseless and senseless claims by the Glasgow brothers.

During a short recess, Shelby related to her mother and Ms. Maude, "Jeb's association with the other two and threats this young man experienced, along with the lack of positive influence from any male relatives, contributed to his criminal involvement. So-called role models who play into young lives by leading them into crime in any country are disgusting. A reason for my desire to educate young people in my county."

The next day after closing arguments, the jury determined verdicts for all three defendants after three short hours. They decided

Hank and Abel Glasgow guilty on all counts. Jeb Clayton was found guilty by failing to report the abduction to the police. He was found innocent of having assisted in the kidnapping and attack against Shelby. The jury believed he tried to stop the confrontation and abduction but was fearful of the Glasgow brothers. Hank and Abel Glasgow had ridiculed themselves by their accusations against Clayton.

After the judge granted her permission to address the court, Shelby took a few seconds to compose herself before facing her abductors. Silence swept over the room while everyone waited. She stared decisively with eyes wide open, her eyebrows raised and spoke determinedly to each of the Glasgow brothers. First looking at one, and then the other.

"I must forgive you for my recovery process," she said, and then paused while eyes focused on Abel and Hank.

The defendants fixed their eyes upon the floor, snickered, and boldly jeered toward one another. Their grinning expressions were an indication made clear to jurors; the Glasgow brothers lacked any account of remorse.

"What I experienced from your threatening and lascivious behavior is too horrific to forget," Shelby said, glaring at the defendants. "I pray the two of you will attempt to better yourselves while incarcerated. Something worth salvaging must exist behind the walls of evil."

They sneered in mockery, inducing a flood of sighs and moans from the courtroom.

Shelby turned to Jeb, took a deep breath, and with marks of grace, spoke softly.

"Jeb, I am sorry you failed to receive the guidance you deserved while growing up. I'm sorry about your involvement. I'm confident you are regretful. I forgive you and will continue to pray for you.

You are smart enough to distinguish the difference between right and wrong. Please learn from this," Shelby waited for his reaction.

Jeb began to shake, uncontrollably sobbing in quick short breaths.

Shelby's voice was calm and direct, "In light of your age and your obvious remorse, I am pleading with Judge Cahill and the court to give you a second chance. I am asking them to consider an opportunity for you to go to school, attend church, and put yourself in a position to make a difference in our community, or the community in which you choose to live,"

Jeb barely squinted through his swollen eyes. His head and body shook as if he were on a vibrating exercise machine. His sobs of painful regret groaned to Shelby's compassion compelled her to walk over and put her arms around him as he poured outcries of remorse. Cameras flashed while Jeb sobbed louder. He begged her forgiveness. The scene was so overwhelming and so unexpected, half the people in the courtroom wiped away tears. Judge Cahill waited several minutes without interrupting.

"What a headline this will make!" members of the press chanted.

Deliberations led to convictions within four hours. Hank and Abel Glasgow received the maximum penalty of life and would become old men before eligible for parole.

"This is one case I am happy to lose," Marvin Jacobs said to his wife. Jury members doubted his faith in words of defense, but he fulfilled his commitment to the fullest.

When young Jeb waited to hear his sentence, Judge Cahill stared at him in stony silence for sixty seconds, and then he spoke straightforwardly, "Young man, Ms. Evans proposes you are a young life worth saving," he waited before continuing. Complete silence dominated the room.

Finally, the judge spoke determinedly, "I am inclined to agree with Ms. Evans. However, finding you guilty by association is something I must consider. I am recommending two years in a learning rehabilitation center. You will face opportunities for schooling you need and guide you missed. You must use this opportunity, and I overemphasize the word 'opportunity' to rebuild your life, rather than as a punishment. Spend your days wisely. The judge emphasized his words without expression, giving Jeb the most lenient sentence considered.

"I want you to understand the testimony of Ms. Evans played a large part in my decision. If not for her, you faced severe punishment. Give in to your intuition of right and wrong. Choose your company wisely."

Reporters scrambled to run stories.

Shelby arrived home to Kentucky and picked up her newspaper to a notable headline mimicking the WASHINGTON POST: ***SECOND CHANCE FOR JEB...*** with an in-depth article including highlights of the Washington trial.

Congratulatory praises from family, friends, and well-wishers poured into Shelby's mail. What she did for Jeb Clayton gave acclaim to applause from numerous well-wishers.

Thirty-Nine

When Shelby began to write again, she wrote about the advantages of education and the importance of role models in young lives.

> ***"I challenge every parent or guardian responsible for the well-being of a child to lead him or her toward productive goals, and to monitor their choices when it comes to choosing friends. Children thrive on the support of their dreams of accomplishment, along with constructive criticism. Nourishing leadership, not only by parents and guardians but by teachers and by community leaders is important. With positive role models, encouragement and opportunities leading them with incentives to excel, they are safer, happier, and better equipped to live productive, successful lives away from temptations and a potential life of crime due to their environment."***

Shelby emphasized how a community can unite in motivating troubled and disadvantaged children and help them to develop skills. The community rallied in support of her documentaries. Families began sharing with one other. Teachers began to understand their students individually comprehensively and by circumstances, rather than categorized by group and textbook descriptions. Shelby's writings brought awareness to families and teachers.

> *"Standard programs designed to meet the needs of students in general, are essential. However, children are individuals who look to adults for guidance and often for help. Our consciousness as parents and teachers can give awareness when a child reveals signs of having been mistreated, abused, bullied, or living in poverty. As a parent or teacher, talking to, and listening to a child, becoming aware of signals indicating pain can save a child from harm or despair. Children are our future."*

Once Shelby regained her full-bodied strength, her mission escalated to proposed visits to the hill country. She had gained momentum because of her sudden notoriety. Those who learned of her project and supported her offered ideas and their willingness to volunteer. Her friend, Kate, organized clothing and food drives for those in need and interviewed qualified volunteers to join an expedition team.

"Enlisting people suitable for this mission depends upon the success of the mission," Kate told Shelby. "Stories of bootlegging and abuse-related by school children who mimicked their parents may merit sensitive issues to investigate."

During a meeting at the Fiscal building, Kate and Shelby convinced council members of the importance to aid people who lived in situations without access to amenities designed for all the county, such as schooling, clinical provisions, and law enforcement.

"If people in the hills are notably without necessary provisions and abandoned to a poverty-stricken exile, and if children are being abused, neglected, or deprived in our community, I see it as a moral and legal responsibility of our community," said Shelby. "According to statistics, life expectancies become a declining factor due to the lack of dental and health advantages.

"I have heard the term, ***'God Forsaken Hill Country',*** God has not forsaken those hills," Shelby professed, "I don't want to forsake them either."

Forty

In early fall, after weeks of preparation, a team of six volunteers with Jake Beasley as their guide determined to meet with inhabitants of an isolated hill country. The group met at a command center positioned at the base of a mountain. Sam Shoney and an off-duty deputy volunteered to stay behind to communicate with the others in case of trouble. The expedition challenged the team to expect the unexpected. Beasley warned the team to be on alert for anyone with a gun, and as a precaution, they wore bulletproof vests concealed under fatigues. A couple of men acquainted with coal miners living in the hills reassured the others of an anticipated friendly greeting by villagers, which elevated their sense of safety.

"However, we may run across someone high-spirited enough to shoot first and ask questions later," Beasley interjected.

The group approached the foothills of a mountain where they reached a deep canyon. They watched as a steady current flowed down from high above, depositing sediment-laden water into a stream below. Jake led them away from the stream and to an overgrown path where they pulled forward up the mountain. They clung to vines for support and stepped over low lying branches. They hiked over large rocks, tree stumps, through broken tree branches, and marsh filled with stalks of reeds until reaching a higher, rocky terrain. They climbed through needle pricking plants, consciously aware of sudden interference by wild beasts. The group prepared for threats from dangerous animals by carrying knives and tranquilizers to use as a defense. After long minutes turned into hours of intense physical exertion, they stopped to rest. They sat upon a plateau, close to a mountain top, and warmed by the sun on a breezy September day. The group admired the spectacular mountain scenery until they saw a tall hillside a short distance away, which had been invaded by bulldozers and tree removal equipment in preparation for strip-mining. Strip mining or contour mining, excavating around mountains or hillsides, destroys the land and is prohibited in select areas. Mountains utilized for strip mining are rarely restored to their original position as required in cases by government officials.

They watched the hill below, knowing a mining company would soon spoil a large area, raising environmental concern, but in contrast, employ out-of-work miners.

After a fifteen-minute rest, they persistently marched toward a village of dwellings known to Beasley.

"Mountains in part of Appalachia are more rugged than Blue Ridge and not as easy to climb. Beasley explained the narrow valleys and sharp ridges of the mountains.

Suddenly, a reddish-brown bobcat with pointed ears rocketed through the matted-down brush, startled them, and with a flash disappeared into the wilderness.

"This is unusual," said Beasley after everyone regained their composure, "Bobcats usually appear at night. Males aren't as territorial as females. That animal didn't mind us being here; it's probably a male. Other animals to become aware of," he said after catching his breath, "are smaller mammals, raccoons, and skunks. Of course, reptiles, an occasional bear, and many deer scamper through these hills."

The group, wild-eyed with concern, especially the women, shuddered, reminded of the dangers. They sensed the bobcat as a reality check.

Beasley and the tender footed civilians pushed their way through a path of a matted down brush when a sudden unexpected change in the weather occurred. A dark cloud of fog hovered, and suddenly a heavy, fast rain began to fall. Everyone stirred and searched for some type of shelter, but rain bounced hard, off surrounding trees.

Forty-One

Without warning, Shelby pushed past Beasley and swiftly moved forward. She had caught a glimpse of a partly obscured house behind a shadowy figure of either a statue or person. She cautiously inched forward toward the dwelling until she faced a woman standing on the porch of a small cabin. The woman, with her eyes trained on Shelby, held a rifle ready to point. Two young children, presumably elementary school-age, hid behind the woman, gripping her skirt.

"We are not here to harm you," Shelby said, and quickly removed homemade loaves of bread and two dozen cookies wrapped in pink cellophane from her backpack. She smiled and pleasantly offered them to the woman.

"I live in town, and I want to talk to you. I want to talk to you about schooling for the little ones."

The petite woman, with mousy brown hair, thick and curly, wore an oversized tattered blue dress. She remained silent and held tightly to her rifle, protective of her children. Shelby wondered if the woman ever owned a new dress. Shelby assumed the woman a middle-aged, a woman about forty-five or fifty years old, but looking at her children, Shelby guessed her as much younger.

Shelby spoke with a calm voice while holding a flat hand up to face the others, motioning them to stay a distance away. The woman stared at Shelby and trained her eyes on the others for several seconds. She slowly lowered her rifle and stood to stare at Shelby and the group. Shelby shivered, drenched from the rain. Torrential raindrops pelleted her face and bare head.

After a few moments longer, the woman beckoned to Shelby, "Come!" She scooted her children inside and motioned for Shelby to follow, ignoring the others.

The woman invited Shelby to sit at a small wooden table. She gave her name as Effie and listened to Shelby tell about school and the benefits of education. Effie stared at her in wonderment. She couldn't understand this pretty, young woman cared enough to climb into the hills to help her and her neighbors. She dreamt of educating her children after she lost her husband, their father.

Soon, Shelby began to win Effie's confidence and asked her if she might introduce some of her friends and bring them out of the rain. Effie invited them onto the sturdy, narrow porch where they began pulling gifts of food and other items out of their backpacks.

After the rains subsided and tensions ceased, Shelby requested Effie to invite some of her neighbors. Several curious women and a couple of men strolled toward Effie's cabin, where the visitors from town introduced themselves and distributed gifts to the people who opened up to the friendly generosities. They told how their primary source of food came from produce grown in the mountains and from wild game. The men either worked in the mine or as avid huntsmen, as well as farmers. They lived in winter by what they managed to store from early crops. Most avoided the town and visited only as a necessity. We are making a tremendous breakthrough; Shelby's smile told the others.

Over the next few weeks, Shelby, along with volunteers from town, visited the hills frequently. They delivered supplies, clothes, and toys for the children, and over time, developed a rapport with most of whom they had met. They provided clothing and blankets for people to keep warm during winter months. Men from town chopped wood for the women and children who were left alone without male figures who had either died or deserted their families by running away. Shelby found the reasons families chose to home-school their children stemmed from having no transportation into town to not having proper clothing. She convinced them of the importance of schooling children in a constructed educational environment and promised to use everything within her power to help. Shelby developed a friendship with Effie and her children, and in time, considered them a priority project. After Effie lost her husband in a mining accident, she hadn't understood if she and her children were entitled to a settlement from the mining company.

"I will look into what happened," Shelby told Effie, "If the company holds an obligation because of the accident, I will contact the appropriate people to retrieve compensation for you and the children."

Careful to avoid embarrassments to a specific group, Shelby wrote a documentary asking for donations and provisions for all people in need in her county. She gave away clothing items from her closet and bought clothes for Effie and her children.

A few men living in the hills relentlessly refused to accept help, but in some cases, their women took a stand and graciously accepted the fellowship of townspeople. Others, both men, and women resisted firmly, unyielding to change. With their lack of conformity unchallenged, some of the people refused to incorporate a change from 'adequate subsistence standards'. Fortunately, everyone with growing children accepted the goodwill of the towns-folk and expressed appreciation.

By all indication, bootlegging had passed from existence with older generations. Evidence of severe abuse or violence within the village as rumored did not exist. If it existed, it existed in the lives of former ancestors. Families lived quietly and undisturbed as their parents and grandparents before them. Although each family had been accustomed to living with firearms, they did not resemble the Hatfield's and McCoy's, feuding and fighting, as rumored. Attitudes from both townspeople and people living in the hills soon improved, having familiarity and understanding of one another.

Women and children outnumbered men living in the hills. Men either died in mines or as one woman described, "They just runned off."

Shelby and Sam worked out a plan with volunteers to clear a better trail leading toward the isolated village before they introduced their ideas to the town council of how to help the people. The council members agreed they should become involved. With individual donations and grants, school busses expanded their routes for easier access to the village affording transportation to children from the hills to schools.

Emergency vehicles soon could disperse to the area when needed. Shelby's influence, efforts by Kate Morley, and countless volunteers made it possible for lives that may have been non-descript before, to flourish. After a short time, people began to enjoy access to the town in which they previously considered off-limits, having reasoned to stay restricted and confined to a lessor environment as their families before them. Men from town volunteered their services to make improvements to cabins in the wilderness. Men in the hills began taking an interest in construction, and by working alongside townspeople developed additional skills other than mining. Women learned sewing and cooking skills from volunteers. Others worked in the school lunchroom to stay close to their children, now enrolled. High-school students cheerfully volunteered to tutor adults to read and write. Life for the hill people steadily improved. They embraced connections to the town and friendships of townspeople. Importantly, their children enjoyed the fellowship of new friends and a controlled learning environment. In time, more people conceded for better conditions, seeing progress in opportunities and friendships. They began to understand the sincerity of townspeople who volunteered their services. In a short time, the townspeople and people living in the hills started to understand and trust one another. Shelby's team had produced a positive effect for all concerned.

Shelby gained favorable recognition for her role in helping people in the county to grow together. National television interviewers frequently invited Shelby to appear on a show. Other communities in rural areas asked for advice, urging her to speak of the importance of educating children in diverse situations. The charisma she had for such a task caused people, young and old, to listen as if she held a particular influence and credibility.

In one of her interviews, Shelby made a statement about her community..."God populates these hills with his people, and if given a chance, success stories not yet told will surface. No one should live forgotten and alone because of a lack of opportunity or lack of access to a broader community. Our neighbors are important," she said with conviction. "People isolated in rural communities are no different from us. Once they are taken out of poverty situations and given a chance to communicate their skills, opportunities will become available. We all experience challenges. It is good to depend upon each other now and then. The key phrase is 'take an interest in your neighbors and surroundings.

"This is an ongoing effort from an assemblage of people. The volunteers who worked diligently and unselfishly are all heroes," Shelby said in her interviews. "These changes are profound and will not happen overnight. In this community, our school system is planning additional classes offering vocational training and occupational therapy to anyone interested, whatever the age. We want to make sure that those who were previously eligible but lacked opportunities for advancement because the privileged received the awards, does not happen. We can expect adjustments and conflicts, but helping people to improve lives through a community effort is beneficial to the community.

"I challenge residents of small towns across America, as I have been challenged, along with my neighbors, expand your willingness to show respect for one another. Treating people in diverse situations as rivals will not improve our relations. Reinforce the growth and education available to your community, volunteer, and share your knowledge. Let's work together to improve relationships, one family at a time, and one county at a time."

"Shelby, your speeches are great," Kate told her. "You should add them to your resume'. You depict the dedication and charisma of a politician and exude the spirit of an evangelist in the right way. In any case, my Christian prayers and my political vote are yours."

"I'll remember that if I set out to run for president or mimic Elmer Gantry," Shelby said. They chuckled.

Shelby persistently made a difference. She earned respect from everyone who came to know her. She was a courageous and spirited young woman with a heart full of compassion. People from other areas began taking their resume's to her county, asking for employment. The community grew with additional healthcare workers, teachers, etc. Through combined efforts of Shelby, Sam Shoney, council members, and anonymous donations, the medical clinic enlarged to accommodate a more significant number of people to visit for treatment, immunizations, etc.

Forty-Three

In middle December, Christopher Stone's flight landed at Sheremetyevo International airport in Moscow. A blast of winter wind left its mark of dreariness in the city. At midnight, Stone and his driver drove along a major highway circling the frigid town until they reached a boulevard leading to the Moscow River, which flowed through the center of the city. The driver pulled up to the Russia Hotel, described as one of the largest hotels in the world. Chris hired him for the duration of his stay in Moscow and asked to have picked him up the next morning.

During long hours in the night, Chris's mind clouded with images of the past and reflections of the future. He began to mutter aloud, "If Maria were here, seeing her father again might solve some of the enigmas. How will I react to meeting the grandfather I never knew and discovering he is possibly my father's killer? How will my family react if it turns out to be true?" He soon fell asleep listening to Russian classical music on the radio.

The next morning, Norty, the English-speaking driver, promptly waited by his cab at the entrance of the hotel for his fare. He tipped his hat and held the door open when Chris approached. They drove along the Moscow River by the Kremlin and the Red Square, through crowded city streets, and past high-rise apartment buildings. Several minutes later, they arrived at a large tenement building, reaching the address Cravens had given to Chris. The high-rise apartment building, isolated in an urban area, cold and lonely, and framed by a vast wooded forest, was home to several Muscovite residents. In Chris's mind, he imaged the home of a lonely dragon.

Norty waited outside as Chris entered the building and walked past a malfunctioning elevator. Musty halls suggested poor ventilation or mold and poorly lighted. Walls painted an institution beige needed repair, and wooden stairs creaked with age. By the time he bravely reached the fourth floor, Chris realized he lacked any conscious knowledge of what he would say as an opening when face to face with his grandfather, who possibly did not know of his existence. He paused for a moment, caught his breath from climbing three flights up the dingy staircase, and firmly knocked on a door displaying black letters in bold print, Unit 4G. Chris prepared to meet his grandfather for the first time, suspecting to confront a killer. Moments later, he listened to shuffling noises before the door opened slightly. An older man, predictably in his eighties, cautiously peered from behind the door. The old man's face illuminated surprise. His icy blue eyes opened wide. He was visibly suspicious of strangers. His forehead wrinkled above a crinkled look when he glared at his visitor, and with words barely audible, he spoke in Russian, which Chris did not understand.

"Mr. Villella?" asked Christopher.

"Yes! Who are you? What do you want?" The man answered in English, unwilling to open the door further.

"My name is Christopher Stone. I am a film producer in the United States. I want to talk over a matter concerning your daughter, Maria. I am seeking answers to questions of which you may be of help. I need to speak with you, please!"

The old man's eyes widened. He stared at his visitor for several seconds, and then he allowed the door to swing open enough for Chris to enter. He wore wrinkled clothes over a body frail and bent, Chris towered over him.

"Please sit," the man guided his visitor toward a plain Formica table and two matching chairs — the neatly furnished apartment with few amenities swathed in depression and loneliness.

In the kitchen, a small sink anchored to the wall and supported by two flimsy metal posts to the floor stood next to an old refrigerator. From the kitchen, Chris glanced toward an opened bathroom door next to a bedroom. In the living area, connecting the kitchen, a tattered brown couch faced a small screen television placed upon a full oak bookshelf against a blank wall. The video, with the sound, turned to mute, mirrored images of a news and weather station. Aside from a signature bottle of Stolichnaya Vodka, which sat unopened on the top shelf of the bookshelf, the apartment presented a meager and lonely dwelling. A far cry from what Chris had imagined from Maria's description of her father as a once sophisticated, popular member of the Russian government. Maria often described living in a home of great wealth and prominence and filled with emptiness.

A view from the window from the living room overlooked the vast loneliness of mighty oak trees wrapped in a blanket of wintry ice. Chris saddened at the absence of Christmas decorations during the season, no wreaths, no tree, nothing to celebrate the festive season. The old man lived isolated and alone.

"What is this about Maria? Is she well?" he asked.

"I am so sorry to inform you, Mr. Villella, but Maria passed away one year ago. She died from injuries in an automobile crash. An attempt to reach her relatives failed."

The gripping news greatly saddened him. He mumbled in Russian and then in English, "No! No! Not my, Maria." The old gentleman sobbed and asked questions about the accident, not wanting to believe this stranger. After Chris explained about the car accident and how she was unable to avoid another driver, he bowed his head for several minutes. When he began to speak, his voice quivered; his bloodshot eyes teared.

Chris had sought anger and resentment toward the Villella, but pity and compassion outweighed any emotion of hatred or resentment. He waited for several moments, allowing his grandfather to collect his composure before he spoke.

"Tell me about yourself," Chris said softly, "Are you here alone? Do you have relatives in Moscow?"

"I have few friends, no relatives, only Maria," the old man said mournfully. "The Russian government excommunicated me from my peers and stripped me of my position after I denounced issues of government," he said, beginning to trust the stranger. "I spent a few years in prison until I pretended to change political opinions. I didn't want Maria to know. These are the reasons I didn't pursue a course to find my daughter."

Villella became audible. He talked about Maria and his deceased wife. What he said confirmed what Chris had learned from Maria, the fact her mother died when Maria was young, and her father, a city government employee, often played chess. Maria, a member of the Bolshoi Ballet, was their only child. The two men talked for an hour.

"Tell me, Mr. Villella, are you aware Maria gave birth to a son?"

"Yes! The child did not live," Villella said.

"Did anyone speak to you concerning what happened to the baby's father?" Chris asked.

"I didn't know any of Maria's suitors, but a gentleman who came to visit told me the man worked as a fisherman and died in a drowning at sea.

"Did he tell you the fisherman's name?"

"No! I don't recall he did, but after he left, I found he had left a paper with a name. I have it here. I will get it for you." The old man disappeared into his bedroom, shuffled around, fumbled, and brought out a yellowed piece of paper with the words, 'Target, Giovanni Sforza.'

Chris's heart banged against his chest. Nausea poured throughout his body. When he gained composure, he said, "The fisherman, Giovanni Sforza, the name on the paper, is the name of Maria's baby's father. An investigation into his death and newly collected evidence suggest murder." Chris stared at his grandfather. He watched his reaction, but Villella did not flinch. He sadly shook his head from side to side.

"Most unfortunate! I had no connection to the man. Maria made her choices and distanced away from family. She came close to destroying her wonderful career opportunity with the Ballet Company," Villella said with disappointment.

"Who are you, and why are you so interested in my daughter?" Villella straightened his shoulders, squared his body toward Chris, and demanded an answer.

Chris turned away and walked to gaze out the window at the sullen trees. Villella sat and waited.

Chris took a deep breath, turned toward the old man, and with remarkable composure and self-control, solemnly affirmed, "Maria's child did not die. Maria is my mother."

Forty-Four

The old man turned pale, "What did you say?" he gasped, "I understood Maria's child died at birth."

"A couple by the name of Stone adopted me when I was a few days old. They perished in a plane crash before Maria's death," said Chris, "I re-connected with Maria when I became twenty-one, and we lived together after she retired from dancing and until the car accident."

Chris hesitated before saying anything further. He watched his grandfather bow his head and stare at the floor for several seconds. When he turned to face Chris, he stood. His chin dipped toward the floor. His legs weakened, and he lumbered toward the couch.

After a long silence, Chris spoke in a mild-mannered tone, "Maria suspected you had a part in the death of my father."

"So, this is why she didn't contact me," the old man grumbled sadly and sat with his head in his hands. He regained his composure, and without blinking, stared at Chris. Chris regarded the Villella's misty blue eyes, mirroring Maria's and detected a definite family resemblance.

"I live with regrets. I've harmed those close to me, but I had no hand in causing your father's death," Villella declared defensively.

"Who, in your estimation, benefitted by Maria returning to the Ballet?" Chris asked.

"No one I know of except for people associated with Bolshoi Ballet Company, but their impeccable reputation, they would not jeopardize."

"Who, specifically told you her child died?" Chris asked.

"The man who came to my house also had visited my work. He identified himself as Alexi Trudeau and asked questions of me. He claimed Maria was his close friend and said he wanted me to know what happened to Maria's lover and her baby. He said I should know Maria returned to the Ballet Company. Maria refused to contact me. I wrote his name down because his questions alerted me to possible dishonesty. When I read the papers about Maria's return to the Ballet, I believed him. I wanted Maria to return to the Ballet, but I didn't interfere. I loved my daughter, but she refused to see me, and then I lost contact with her. I did not know her location.

"What about the investigation into the fisherman's death?" he quietly asked.

"The investigation is on-going, and in the hands of the authorities. I expect a trial to proceed in Florence," Chris told him, "I must tell you, you, the evidence points to you as a suspect."

His grandfather stared at Chris in disbelief. His eyes still watered as a man stricken with grief. He sauntered toward the window and stared out at the somber, hanging branches through a shadow of darkness. And then his expression dulled as if blotting out what Chris had said.

"I've killed no one," he said quietly, not in a challenging manner as if attempting to defend himself. Chris saw him as someone with dark sadness, depressed, a beaten man. After a long silence between them, he spoke directly to Chris without a blink.

"If you are my grandson, I am sorry not to have known and sad you lost your parents. I wish you success in finding what happened to your father," A long pause and… "I will miss my adoring wife and my sweet Maria forever."

Chris stayed for another hour and compassionately talked to his grandfather. He considered him a lonely man hibernating in the existence of deep depression. And now, realizing responsible for adding to the older man's depression, sought to comfort the old gentleman. The shock of discovering news of his daughter's death, having met a grandson he did not know existed, and a blowing reality he is a murder suspect of thirty years before that is about to come to life at a trial, overwhelmed the old man.

"Shelby has so much flesh in her editorials," Sam Shoney told his wife after he read one of Shelby's articles before publication. "She writes with enthusiasm about human interest and has so much excitement on how to take on and accomplish what others deem impossible. Shelby has an uncanny way to visualize a solution before others figure out the problem. To employ the words of a journalist, 'she is a lass of nettle.' We may find keeping her hidden in this obscure community, challenging." Sam's gentle voice mirrored disappointment in the possibility of losing Shelby but proud enough to want the best for his talented co-worker who had become much more to him and his wife, more as a daughter.

Shelby continued to visit the Standish farm. She spent time helping in the kitchen and listened while Ms. Maude talked about her life and experiences while living in England. They spoke of family and shared recipes. Shelby helped farmhands tend to the animals. She loved grooming and riding the horses and alternated between two, a four-year-old bay colt and the other, her favorite, a two-year-old chestnut filly well suited for running.

One lonely Sunday afternoon, Chris called Shelby, updating a plan to extend a stay in Italy. They talked about her job, the school, the farm, and Jason's movie. She assumed his business in

Italy involved family or business matters. He didn't elaborate and didn't mention going to Moscow. During their conversation, Shelby learned Jason had rekindled a courtship with his co-star, Sunni.

"This is good," she told Chris. "The short time Sunni and I spent together, I found her to be quite suitable as a match for Jason. They share the same interests and are the same age. How wonderful."

"I am in total support, dear Shelby, but I can't say the same for Ms. Lana. She continues to try and mold her son's future".

Conversations between Shelby and Chris became consistently meaningful, with intense feelings of emotion. He didn't lace his sentences with words of love, but she sensed ripples of passion in his voice.

After she hung up the phone, she thought about his affectionate tenderness, his gentleness, and consideration for others. "I am lucky to have him in my life," she smiled.

Between calls from Chris that Shelby looked forward to, her boundless activities continued to chain events, turning wheels. The following days she spent her spare time at the farm or the high school with the Saturday morning journalism class she organized for adults. Sometimes at home, she dabbled in paints producing another landscape to send to her parents. Unbeknownst to her peers, Shelby had an eye for art and always loved to paint, but not a promoter of her work. She praised other artists, but to her, her work was amateurish in comparison.

"Painting is my hobby. I paint for therapy, a little relaxation," she confessed to those familiar with her work.

Forty-Six

One late winter afternoon, Shelby drove to the farm and went directly to the stable where one of the farmhands helped to saddle the chestnut filly for her. She returned from riding to find Ms. Maude standing outside the barn, emotionally distressed. Tears streamed over her pale cheeks, and her eyes puffed like muffin tops. She clutched a navy-blue shawl wrapped around her shoulders close to her throat.

"What on earth has happened," Shelby yelled as she ran toward her. She feared someone was injured, maybe worse. Has Chris suffered an accident while abroad?"

"No one is hurt. I am dead," Ms. Maude cried, shivering from the cold, "Mr. Chris," she sobbed, and held out a copy of a tabloid magazine she picked up from the market. On the front page…***Ms. Lana Carlina, twice nominated the best actress in Global awards, to wed director, producer, Christopher Stone."***

Shelby froze. She stared at a lone photograph of Lana looking more exotic than she remembered.

Ms. Maude grumbled through sobs as the two of them stared at the caption.

Shelby read the headline in disbelief. She remained stunned for long minutes. "Her legs weakened. She started to shake with tremulous wavers. She felt her heart plunge as if it had shattered into millions of pieces.

"Why?" questioned Ms. Maude. "He has deliberately, as we English say, made a foolish cock-up."

Ms. Maude consistently and verbally rejected the notion of such a union, "I will not stay and serve such an undeserving woman," she said.

" Now, Ms. Maude," Shelby's voice crumbled, "if this is what will make him happy..." she didn't finish. Shelby turned away, hoping to hide the tears welling in her eyes.

Once inside the farmhouse, Ms. Maude instantaneously pulled out the cognac. Shelby stared at the glass for long moments before speaking.

"I am starting to equate cognac with Lana Carlina," she said to Ms. Maude. They both laughed and cried together.

Why does he continue to send flowers to me? Shelby wondered.

"I will wait until Mr. Chris returns home. If he brings Ms. Lana here, I will give my resignation," she said to Shelby, eyebrows lowered, "I will take care of this place until..."

Shelby steered her away from the subject and began to talk about the farm, new recipes, school children, her job, anything to distract from the obvious 'elephant in the room.' Once she saw Ms. Maude had calmed down, she told her she must leave to work on a project. She walked briskly to her truck, where she quietly sobbed, brokenheartedly numbed by grief.

In the following days, the announcement in the magazine of Chris's wedding became a stark reality to Shelby. She believed Chris's interest in her amounted to nothing more than a sham and realized her interest in him meant more to her than she allowed to understand. She had found the man of her dreams too late. She made excuses to cut short conversations when he called her office, claiming to be busy or to answer another call, etc.

She attempted to concentrate on her work and public involvement. Several newspaper editors, including her previous editor in Chicago, courted her for positions. A national television station asked to interview Shelby for a news anchor position. She had become a noted celebrity. Group leaders began to approach her for speaking engagements. She agreed to meet with some when her schedule permitted.

Ms. Maude refused to acknowledge the wedding announcement to anyone. She avoided the subject when Chris called. She never asked about his wedding plans or expressed congratulations to him.

"Mr. Chris is still in Italy on business, and he says he is unable to reach you, dear," Ms. Maude said to Shelby, "He sounds quite worried about you." Her young friend's body language confirmed what Maude had already suspected.

"I'm swamped. Please give Chris my best."

Ms. Maude turned away and sighed of disgust over the engagement. Ms. Maude and Sam Shoney knew the reason for Shelby's personality change but said nothing.

Shelby spent long hours between the school and the newspaper office. She obsessed with keeping her mind clear of what she explained to Kate as 'unreasonable haunts.'

"This is an opportunity for me to leave town and get away from the farm before Chris returns from abroad," she told her friend.

One late afternoon in December, Shelby was actively busied by decorating a small Christmas tree. She startled when her phone rang. Anticipating Chris, on the other end, she prepared not to answer, but the caller identification gave the name of a detention center in Indiana. Shelby remembered having given her number to a counselor in the event of a problem. She quickly picked up the phone, not knowing what to expect. When Jeb answered, her negative expectation of bad news promptly faded.

"Hello, Ms. Evans, this is Jeb Clayton," he said. "I followed your advice and am getting an education. I am working hard to pass my GED and am learning a lot from the chaplain here. Because of you, I plan to work toward becoming a reporter," he paused a long silence as if waiting for her approval. "I wanted to tell you how grateful I am to you. You are a role model in my life, and I wanted to let you know," his young voice stirred with emotion. He was unsure of her response.

She delighted to hear him speak with improved grammar. He spoke with a distinct characteristic expression. He sounded mature, nothing like the boy at the trial.

"Jeb, thank you so much for keeping me informed. I am proud of the progress you are making."

They talked for a few moments. Shelby listened to Jeb intently while he apologized for his involvement during the abduction. After completing the call with a promise to stay in touch, she pledged to continue to monitor his development. She sat eased back in a relaxed chair, and with a satisfied smile, justified the decision she and the judge had agreed upon for Jeb Clayton's rehabilitation.

"A life worth saving," she said aloud and sighed as if relieving responsibility of her decision to address the court on his behalf.

She listened to pleasant upbeats of Christmas carols from classical masterpieces while she decorated her Christmas tree. Suddenly, she startled by the ring of the doorbell. A courier presented her with a large poinsettia and an endearing card, signed, ***Affectionately, Chris.***

"Why does he insist on send flowers?" she scowled.

When her parents called, her Mom detected somehow the Yuletide season had failed to capture Shelby's heart.

"Will you visit with us for a few days during the holidays, dear?"

"Mom, I'd love to, but Ms. Maude is alone. She will not leave the farmhouse unattended. I stay with her on weekends while she is alone. Ms. Maude looks forward to baking for the farmhands during the holidays, and I plan to help her with decorations.

"Of course, we understand, dear. We will miss you, perhaps later," Shelby and her mother mutually agreed.

Forty-Seven

With her workweek full of activity, Shelby began to develop a quiet, modest demeanor and attempted to change her mind and accept what she must. She spoke as an advocate for the people in the hills and counseled townspeople who asked for advice or assistance. She had become a sounding board to those who found her approachable and with a compassionate heart. Many merely expressed their grievances over the town council, school system, etc., and often attempted to offer solutions to fit their needs. She listened to the worthy and the ridiculous, and always extended a polite reply as a counselor.

Shelby and her friend, Kate, joined the students in decorating the gymnasium for the holiday festivities during the week. On the weekend, Shelby bought gifts for Effie and her two children and invited them to her cottage for lunch and a small pre-Christmas celebration. She would enjoy taking them to the farm to visit the animals but remembered Chris's unyielding adamancy in refusing strangers to the farm.

Shelby realized Effie's determination to live a better life and to school her children. She helped her set a goal to relocate into town closer to school and tutored her in the underlying protocol, English, reading, and writing. She taught her the fundamentals of makeup and gave her clothes in which to present a professional appearance when applying for work. Effie became a quick study, and with Shelby's help, set goals. She worked hard to plan a better life where she was better able to care for her children.

Shelby helped Effie win a settlement from the mining company where Effie's husband worked at the time of his accidental death. The accident occurred due to a significant equipment malfunction, which proved neglect by the company. With the monies she received, Effie bought a small bungalow in town. She began looking her age, as a young mother instead of an over-worked, aging servant.

The following week, Shelby found the farm exceptionally quiet when she arrived preparing to stay over the weekend. She looked forward to seeing Ms. Maude and help with decorating. They exchanged holiday recipes, and Ms. Maude entertained Shelby by telling her stories of her childhood. She spoke of how she worked for one of the royal families until moving to the United States to be closer to a brother, now deceased.

"Mr. Chris and Jason were my only family until you came along, love. I am afraid of what the future might bring with Mr. Chris," she sobbed as if grieving over a lost relative.

"Ms. Maude, Mr. Chris, regards you as a dear relative. He would suffer without you, as would Jason. You must wait, things will work out. Lana may choose to live in California for the greatest amount of time. I can't picture her milking cows and slopping hogs."

Before Ms. Maude caught her breath from laughing, Jason burst through the door without warning. He grabbed onto both.

"Jason?" they both exclaimed with joy and curiously peeked behind him.

"Sorry, Chris is still in Italy," he said. "I came to get good food, and I find my two favorite girls in the kitchen, life doesn't get much better."

"Why didn't you call?" Shelby scolded, "I would've picked you up."

Ms. Maude held him tight and sobbed for joy, "What about your mum?" she asked.

"Lana has business to attend. She will plan big for her wedding," he said to Ms. Maude. "Expect a lavish wedding. I wouldn't be surprised if she asked me to dress as a Tasmanian ring bearer."

The two women failed to laugh at the humor in any part of Chris's and Lana's wedding and said nothing.

"What's with the gloom, you two? I thought you were happy to see me."

"We are!" Shelby interrupted; we're hoping you can stay for a while."

"I will stay through Christmas Eve," he said.

"Wonderful love!" Ms. Maude said joyfully, still holding his hand. "I will enjoy time to fatten you up," she squinted and patted his belly with motherly affection.

Jason turned to Shelby, his eyebrows raised, "Chris is disappointed he is unable to reach you, Shelby. He is fond of you and is worried. What is the matter?" he asked bluntly.

She turned away and went into her dog and pony rendition of how busy she has been, while Ms. Maude simply replied in her typical English tone, "Rubbish!"

Shelby gave no other excuse.

Jason's puzzled expression changed to concern when he and Shelby relaxed over a glass of wine, giving Ms. Maude a chance to put finishing touches on dinner.

"Shelby, did anything go wrong with the sentencing in Washington?" Jason asked. He determined to find why her mood changed so drastically.

"No!" she sighed, "the two brothers denied involvement. In the end, they got what they deserved, life. If freed, the court believes they will kill again. Our local authorities are collecting evidence tied to them, suggesting they killed before. They are investigating a couple of unsolved cases."

"I am sorry not to have been present to support you at the trial," he said apologetically. "Chris was there to represent both of us. Unfortunately, his demanding schedule prevented him from staying. He disappointedly left when he failed to get close enough to talk to you. He said a group of reporters surrounded you."

He paused for a moment and said..." One of the women, identified as someone with whom you worked alongside previously, told him your boyfriend came in for the trial."

Jason waited for her response with a proverbially inquisitive expression.

"Chris's being in the courtroom meant a lot to me. I missed spending time with him. Tony is a former boyfriend and still a friend," she explained. "I didn't expect him."

"Oh! Chris assumed you renewed a relationship with someone before moving to Kentucky, a little competition." Jason's inquiries wouldn't stop. He remained inflexible.

She glared at him in disbelief. Competition? Competition, indeed, she mumbled under her breath. What is the difference if Chris has competition, and why hasn't he been forthcoming?

"No, we stopped dating a long time ago, before I moved to Kentucky," she said calmly. "We remained friends."

The two continued a friendly chat. Shelby avoided asking him anything about his mother's wedding plans or where she and Chris planned to reside. Her mood changed to an upbeat when she began talking about young Jeb Clayton and her hopes for him.

"Jeb talked to me from the detention home. I sincerely expect he is trying to change his life. He has goals, not in his vocabulary before."

"Good news! So, what else did I miss? What is your next project, and what are the goals you set for yourself?"

Forty-Eight

"I am interviewing for an anchor position in Maryland," she told him. The opportunity is sound, and maybe a change might relieve some stress from the past. What is your opinion?"

Confiding in Jason always came easy for Shelby. The two bonded as siblings. Charming to her was his modest demeanor, which remained unpretentious, unlike the stereo Hollywood stars, including that of his mother.

"From what I read about you in past weeks, the job and price are yours for the asking. Your heart is here as mine is. I picked up a lot from working with you at the farm and studying your television interviews. When you speak of this town and its people, your face glows.

"Your role in liberating the hill people is an inspirational influence throughout the country. Whatever you decide, I hope you visit the farm often and always stay in touch," he said genuinely.

His words harvested more maturity than she remembered. Shelby, unable to speak, reached over and hugged him, overcome with emotion and his unwavering friendship. He hugged her back without saying a word, and the two of them entered the dining room at Ms. Maude's request.

The weekend soon came to an end. Shelby prepared to go home and make her schedule for work for the next day, when, "Shelby, Chris is on the phone. He wants to wish all of us a Merry Christmas. He is calling from Italy." Jason stared directly at Shelby and decidedly held the phone toward her.

Shelby hesitated. Caught completely off guard, Shelby walked toward Jason, paused, took in a deep breath, and with a trembling hand, reached for the phone.

She suffered extreme emotional discomfort, but spoke with a steady voice, "Hello."

"Shelby, how are you, my dear? I miss talking to you. I miss you."

"I'm well, Chris. I'm keeping busy these days. I visit Ms. Maude on weekends when I can. She takes good care of me." The tone of her voice favored a vague summary of an itinerary, unfamiliar to him. He reached out in pleasant conversation, longing for the intimate warmth he remembered.

"What is going on with your job at the paper and the school," he asked. He expressed pride in Shelby's interests and accomplishments, having told her on numerous occasions.

"Everything is coming along smoothly," she said. Her resistance for feeling toward Chris remained brusque, bordering on rude.

He wondered if the trial experience had caused a shattering impact on her.

"Shelby, please take care of yourself. You are most important to me."

Disappointed by her lack of enthusiasm, Chris ended the call, perceiving disinterest. They said their goodbyes after a brief and unassuming conversation.

"Maybe she is depressed. I must talk this over with Ms. Maude when I return to the States," Chris mumbled somberly, with his eyes fixed outside the window at his aunt's home. He stared, with blurred vision, at the enormous moon showering over a field of suburban villas and made assumptions to account for her mood change.

How can he say such a thing, how can I be most relevant to him? What about his betrothed? Isn't Lana most important? Chris's remark upset Shelby even more.

Ms. Maude listened and shook her head from side to side at the determination of self-control and pride in Shelby's voice.

Forty-Nine

Shelby said her goodbyes to Ms. Maude and Jason and hurried to her truck before she broke into tears. Jason attempted to escort her but too late. He lingered outside for several minutes, watching her vanish in a cloud of dust on the narrow country road. He waited, silent and confused until a flatbed truck disappeared behind her. Jason's curiosity about her behavior increased. He pledged to get to the bottom of whatever bothered her.

"Ms. Maude, is Shelby ill? She doesn't seem her spunky self." Maude simply shrugged her shoulders and began tidying up the kitchen.

At home, Shelby's low spirits of melancholy and sadness swept over her. She longed for a relationship beyond her reach. She vowed to overcome disappointment and heartbreak.

As Christmas approached, Ms. Maude busied herself in the kitchen, preparing treats for the farmhands and a special Holiday celebration for Jason and Shelby. Jason, on the other hand, assisted in mucking stalls, feeding the animals, and clean-up in and around the barns.

"Jason doesn't mind filth and grime," one of the farmhands told Ms. Maude. He pitches right in cleaning up barnyard manure with the rest of us."

"He is one in a million, nothing like his Mum," Ms. Maude said with fixed emotion.

The night of Christmas Eve, Ms. Maude prepared a Christmas feast. Jason played the piano, and the three of them sang Christmas Carols. Jason viewed Shelby in a happier light, like her old self, which pleased him. Chris called again and gratefully found Shelby less reserved than before. She didn't understand why Lana failed to enter the phone conversation but didn't ask. Maybe Lana hadn't accompanied him to Italy, she thought.

The next morning, Ms. Maude outdid herself again with a brunch fit for kings. Afterward, they exchanged gifts. Shelby's gift to Jason was a lifelike oil painting of his favorite horse, a full-grown stallion named Niagara.

"Shelby, this is fantastic. I didn't realize the paintings in your cottage were yours. I am in awe of your artistic nature among your other talents; I want you to exhibit."

"Thank you, Jason. About that. I exhibited some work in my hometown, and an art connoisseur in New York became interested in evaluating my work. He saw photographs of my paintings the local art dealer had sent to him and requested some of the paintings. I am quite excited, but don't have high expectations.

"I like to dabble in paint," she said modestly and presented a beautiful piece she painted for Chris. The painting viewed the farmhouse home at a slight angle, with a partial view of the giant barn and a breathtaking view of the meadow. The tall oak trees in front of the house, the landscaping, the towering pillars, windows, and flowering pink and white dogwoods emphasized unique distinction. The painting compared to what could be mistaken for a photograph taken on a beautiful spring morning.

"Shelby, this is without a doubt, a masterpiece. Your talent is incredible," Jason professed and confirmed by Maude.

"Please let us know the minute you hear from the art dealer."

"Yes, of course, I will."

Shelby's gifts to Ms. Maude included a splendid set of shiny new carving knives. Ms. Maude had commented about the dull knives in her kitchen. Other gifts from Shelby, included Ms. Maude's favorite fragrance and a bottle of the forever" healing" cognac.

Jason presented the little English housekeeper with a gift certificate to Harrods, a fitting gift to use when she visits her homeland to visit with her friends, a vacation gift from Chris.

"For you, my dear Shelby," Jason said, "Chris and I combined our ideas and came up with the same one. Look out the window. The gift is from both of us.

"What in the world?" she muttered as she peered through the shutters. To her surprise, a filly with a luxurious coat of white elegance, more beautiful than she might imagine, stood outside through the large window at the side of the house. Shelby smiled a broad smile, went out, and as if on cue, the horse whinnied, giving her a unique greeting. Shelby gazed silently at the young filly who reminded her of whipped cream and whose fluffy mane glistened as pure silk. She watched her long and flowing tail flow like a mountain stream. She was speechless.

"Oh, no!" she protested, "I cannot accept this." Jason ignored her and helped her to climb bareback on the filly.

Ms. Maude and Jason smiled at one another.

"You must name her," he announced, "She cannot go back. We pulled too strings to get her here."

"How in the world did you pull this off?" she asked.

"Chris has a lot of connections," he said proudly.

Shelby wondered what to make of Jason's comment about Chris's connections. Why does Chris act this way? He surely doesn't want me around after his marriage. He knows Lana's attitude toward me, or any woman interested in him or Jason. Maybe they don't plan to stay here often, she reasoned.

"This is an expensive gift, Jason," she said.

"You're worth it," he said, smiling ear to ear.

Shelby trotted the filly around, talked to her, tenderly smoothed her mane, and fell in love, while Jason snapped photographs. The graceful horse soon took precedence over her thoughts of the overwhelming disappointment of rejection. After a visit aboard the filly, Shelby, along with Jason, led her into a freshly cleaned stall.

Later in the day, when the time came for Jason to say his goodbyes and return to California, he hugged a tearful Maude and prepared to leave with Shelby for the airport.

"So, therefore, you didn't want me to pick you up," Shelby said, glaring at Jason, "You came with the horse."

"Just horsing around," he said. They both laughed.

Later in the evening, while home alone, Shelby attempted to psychoanalyze why she hadn't won Chris's heart. Maybe if I had spent more time with him, or perhaps it wasn't meant to happen.

Her tormented conclusions failed to give her comfort. Wiping away tears, she began writing a sincere heartfelt thank-you note to each, Chris and Jason, and to Ms. Maude, who loaded her down with food delicacies.

Before bedtime, she began munching on Christmas treats from Ms. Maude. "Now, look at me, I am gorging with food, convincing myself I am not worthy or appealing. Is this what a rejected woman does?" she complained.

She pondered on whether to accept the horse and what name to choose. "After all, the gift is from the two of them, which is less personal," she reasoned before finally drifting off to sleep.

Fifty

Chris celebrated Christmas with his cousins, their families, and Aunt Gina in Florence. They discussed his visit with his grandfather and whether to turn over incriminating evidence in Craven's possession to the Italian authorities.

"I see him as is broken and alone, I don't imagine he ventures out often," Chris told Cravens about the old man. "He hardly fits the legendary Gestapo figure I expected. My grandfather may have been abrasive in his younger days but didn't appear to me as anyone defiant or capable of violence. He didn't respond like a man riddled with the guilt of murder when I brought the subject up. I'm confident he wasn't told of my existence, Maria's death, or believed my father's death was anything but an accident at sea. Before I left, he asked for my contact information, which I gave him.

"The truth has to come out. We must continue with the investigation."

"Are you sure?" his aunt Gina asked. "This may become unpleasant for you."

"Yes!" Chris answered firmly, "All of us deserve to know the truth. We're too far into the investigation. A man's life is in the balance, my family member. Villella is not the imperious tyrant I suspected to find," he told his family. "I found him somewhat frail and broken. If he is innocent, we must make sure he is vindicated. If he is responsible, which I doubt, I want to know. My father deserves justice," He paused and waited for the others to respond, "Are we in agreement?"

They all spoke affirmatively, and Chris asked Cravens to present his findings to authorities for further scrutiny.

"By the way, on a good note, if all goes well, I hope to plan a wedding soon. I want to bring all of you, the entire family to the celebration.

Chris's information about his wedding brought excitement and a cheerful break to everyone.

"It is time for good news, Josef said." They all embraced their beloved cousin and nephew.

"We are so excited for you; you must tell us all about her," his aunt said.

"Yes! Of course," he smiled.

During the evening in Rome at his Aunt's villa, Chris prepared for a restful evening when his aunt Gina knocked on his door with a bottle of her best Chianti. She explained the wine came from Sangiovese grapes from Tuscany in central Italy.

When the two sat down to toast his wedding, she surprised him by presenting her mother's, his paternal grandmother's engagement ring to him. A deep red Ruby encircled by precious diamonds, in an antique setting. The ring, one of a kind, sparkled with the brilliance of an effervescent dewy bubbly with countless gleaming gems.

"Aunt Gina, I can't accept this. The ring is exquisite and expensive," he said.

"Nonsense, I want this for you. Your grandmother would agree. The ring is significant in my parent's relationship. They lived happily married for over 60 years. This symbol of their relationship will bring you and your bride much happiness together. I was never married. Therefore, I pass on to you your grandmother's ring and wish for happiness.

Fifty-One

Days passed. Shelby peered out the window on a Saturday morning, expecting an inspirational surge of warmth. Instead, she suffered guilt for not visiting with her parents over the Holidays. She fought the concept of rejection from Chris and further guilt by holding onto the gift horse. Her shame for desiring the affection of Christopher Stone as a lover annoyed her, "What is wrong with me? I am harboring a lust for someone betrothed to another," she said aloud.

On her laptop, she began searching obtrusively for information on Christopher Stone or Standish, 'or whatever his birth name was.'

While researching news articles from abroad, Shelby read a documentary by a French journalist, Pierre Boulud. The report, recently published by International Weekend, a popular newspaper based in London England, presented Boulud's outline of a feature story with earmarks toward a book he intends to publish. The expose' shows a factual account of a young couple in love, and separated by the mysterious death of a Mediterranean fisherman:

"Giovanni Sforza, a fisherman, and Maria Villella, a young aspiring Russian ballet dancer, met when Villella spent a holiday in Italy while touring with a ballet troupe. After their friendship developed into a romantic relationship, Maria became pregnant.

The link cut short after Sforza drowned in a suspicious fishing incident at sea. Villella, cast off by family and peers after her pregnancy became known, was forcibly convinced to give her child up for adoption. Rumors of the child, having been stillborn, tormented the family. Speculation that the child, born Christopher Fabian Sforza, surfaced later in life under another name, and is known as a prominent member of the American Film Industry in the United States and is in search of his biological father's actual cause of death. Is this truth or unsound speculation? More to be revealed.

"Is this the man who invaded my cogitative dreams?" she said aloud,"What is the rest of the story? Is Chris in Italy to investigate his father's death?" Shelby stared at the picture of Maria Villella. "She is the pretty woman in the painting hanging over the bed in the pink room. Who adopted Chris? She mumbled. He doesn't speak of his parents; I wonder why. How did his mother die? If his visit to Italy is personal, what does it mean? Chris's beginning is a real live movie, at the least."

Bedazzled by what she learned, Shelby groped through the uncertainty of clues to yet another mystery. This new knowledge of Christopher Stone has surfaced with a third name, Sforza.

Suddenly, she jumped at the sound of a loud bell, "Oh, my goodness, I don't remember the doorbell ringing that loud before," she said.

Turning past the window, she peered through the glass pane before opening the door to a postal delivery man. He held a large box from none other than Christopher Stone. Now, what is he up to? She mumbled while signing the receipt. The return postmark on the package revealed a postmark from Southern Europe. He's not letting me forget him too quickly, and what about Lana? Is she concerned about his attention toward me? Is that what Hollywood people are about?

The delivery man left Shelby to mumble and complain. She cut the top off the box, exposing one exquisitely carved, Italian leather, sepia-toned saddle. Another box contained a gold-toned rider's helmet, specially selected to complement her features and coloring.

"I cannot continue to accept these expensive gifts and flowers from him when he is committed to someone else," she said, looking into her mirror at the helmet placed upon her head. "Why must he continue sending expensive gifts?" She returned the helmet into the box and sunk back, relaxed in her desk chair, and studied past happenings.

With a heavy workweek ahead after the Holidays, Shelby began to absorb in her writings. As her work schedule intensified, she thankfully resisted thinking about Chris and what she called 'delusional insanity.'

Friday afternoon, Shelby readied to go to the farm and ride the little gift filly. With the helmet and saddle neatly tucked away in the shipping box, she gathered sweet delicacies from Bonnie's bakery to take to Ms. Maude. The two developed a camaraderie of sorts with questions of why Chris chose to marry Lana after having known her for years, and especially since his obvious affection for Shelby was apparent to everyone.

"Why now?" The concept baffled Ms. Maude. She knew her employer better than any and detected his affection for Shelby was like no other. She didn't understand his reasoning.

"I will reprimand him when he arrives home," Ms. Maude mumbled.

One of the farm-hands anticipated Shelby's visit and saddled the filly before she arrived.

"What shall I call you," Shelby asked the horse, staring into her deep brown eyes. The filly whinnied and tossed her head, allowing her mane to spread in a feathery frame covering down the back of her neck — the two connected as if struck by a fairy's magic wand.

The farmhand leaned against the barn door, smiled, and said aloud, "That is what I call true love."

What a marvelous release, to gallop through open fields with my hair blowing lissome as a feathery wand in a gentle breeze, Shelby thought. Her attachment to the magnificent filly triumphantly inspirited her mood. When they returned to the barn, Shelby gave the little horse a treat from a bucket and spent an hour brushing her coat and talking to her.

Later, in Ms. Maude's kitchen, the two women enjoyed a quiet dinner and, afterward, a touch of the habitually curative cognac.

"Ms. Maude, what about Chris's mom. What happened to her?" she questioned, unwilling to give away what she learned On-Line, "Does he have family who will attend his wedding?"

"None in the United States, Love," she said, "his Mum met with a terrible accident, right before Mr. Chris purchased this farmland and built this magnificent house. Losing his mum nearly killed Mr. Chris," she sadly explained.

"What happened?" Shelby asked, eyebrows raised.

"Mr. Chris bought his mum a new sports car after she retired from dancing. Two weeks later, a drunk driver swerved and hit the two of them on one of the mountain curves in the hills of Los Angeles. His mum persisted in driving, but Mr. Chris blamed himself for not being behind the wheel until his mum became familiar with the road and the car. He believed his instincts and knowledge of the area would've helped to avoid the accident. Mr. Chris went into seclusion. He moved here and attempted to block the entire accident from his mind. He holds the memory of her in the painting in the pink room. I suspect he decorated the room to remind him of her."

"How tragic," Shelby said sorrowfully. "Was he injured?"

"Yes, he spent weeks in the hospital with several fractures but being alive added to his guilt. The other driver and Ms. Maria were the only fatalities. He confided in me once; he remains haunted by seeing her slumped over the wheel with her neck twisted. He experienced nightmares for months but didn't say much. I listened to him at night, stumbling out to the corral, talking to himself. The last time I heard him so distressed was the night before you came to us, all bloody and scared. He had returned from Italy the day before with the painting of his mum. I thanked God for bringing you to us. You are the medicine he needed. Knowing he has a deep affection for you is why I can't understand him now, with Ms. Lana."

"What about his adoptive parents?"

"Before Mr. Chris's mother died, his adoptive parents perished in a catastrophic international plane crash over Egypt, which added to his heartbreak.

"They were a couple connected to an American circus. The Stone's adopted Mr. Chris when he was a few days old and gave him their name, Stone. They loved him and enabled him with the best education available. The Stones stayed in touch with Ms. Maria and introduced the mother and son, face to face after Mr. Chris became twenty-one."

The Stones connected to circus animals! That's why he has such an attachment to animals," Shelby thought.

"What about his father?" she asked.

"Mr. Chris's father died in a fishing accident before Mr. Chris was born. He visits with relatives when he goes to Italy."

Shelby sat in silence. What Ms. Maude had told her confirmed the story she had read. She wrinkled her forehead in deep concentration and numbly sipped the cognac. Ms. Maude's narration affected Shelby's attachment to Chris with warmth and affection.

The two women sat motionless as if meditating. Shelby, intrigued by Ms. Maude's narrative of Chris's life, was overcome by her tearful explanation of Maria's death. She regretted having caused the housekeeper to remember such sadness. Shelby reached over and held her in a loving embrace for several seconds. Shelby realized Ms. Maude solemnly remembered the affection she held for Maria.

Moments later, Ms. Maude broke the spell, "Did you enjoy your ride on the filly, love? Have you decided on a name?"

"I did come up with a few names. I read how the Yukon River Rapids in Canada resembles the mane of a white horse. The capital of Yukon is named Whitehorse. Also, I like the name Holly because of Christmas or maybe Christmas Rose after an evergreen, which produces white flowers in winter."

"Any suggestions?" she asked Ms. Maude, "I am open to names from which to choose." Shelby, suddenly quiet for a moment, staring with her glazed eyes into the meadow.

"What is the matter, dear?" Ms. Maude asked. "Are you ill?"

"No! I'm not ill," she said. I'm not deserving of the horse. I have mixed emotions. I'm attached to her and haven't decided I should keep her."

"Don't be hard on yourself, love, I saw instant affection for you and the little filly," Ms. Maude told her, "You must keep her!" she commanded with authority. The names you chose are lovely. Why not ask children at school to vote on which name they like?"

"Thanks, Ms. Maude, what a great idea. I will quiz the children," she said.

The two busied, cleaning up the kitchen when the phone rang.

"Shelby, will you answer the phone, please?" Ms. Maude asked, wiping her hands.

Fifty-Two

"***What a pleasant*** surprise to hear your voice, dear," Chris said enthusiastically, "Are you and Ms. Maude enjoying the evening?"

"Yes, by all means. We discussed names for the little filly, and Ms. Maude came up with a suggestion to include children at the school in choosing a name.

"What a wonderful idea," he said approvingly.

"Chris, I wish you wouldn't send me expensive gifts. I am preparing to return the saddle and helmet. I cannot continue to accept gifts from you in light of the situation."

"What situation, dear? I realize a proper courtship is not feasible with the distance between us, but you are constantly on my mind. Please keep the saddle and helmet. I would grieve for you to return them," he said.

Shelby listened in disbelief. Courtship? Courtship indeed! And proper? She hardly breathed. What is going on here? Is he in denial of his upcoming marriage, or is this a kind of unsavory understanding the two of them planned out, such as an open marriage? Is this part of his character? She questioned. However, after hearing the unsettling account of how Chris lost his beloved mother, she continued a pleasant conversation with him. She agreed to keep the gifts, silently assuring it was temporary.

Chris gave her a resourceful up-date of Jason's film but said nothing about his investigation in Italy. He had openly confided in no one concerning his business in Italy except Jason.

"Jason should finish in a few weeks. We will arrive at the same time."

Shelby's mind wandered with questions such as who will arrive at the farm. She gave Ms. Maude an account of the conversation, leaving out the mention of 'proper courtship.'

For the remainder of the weekend, Shelby spent her time riding, exchanging stories with farmhands, and grooming horses.

Several requests for speaking engagements, job opportunities, etc. interrupted her routine at the newspaper office during the following work week. Sam, jokingly, offered to act as her secretary and screen her calls. On Friday afternoon, after teaching her journalism class at school, Shelby confided in Kate by giving her a brief description of her last conversation with Chris.

"Shelby, possibly something else is going on. Why not swallow your pride and ask about his marriage to Lana? Confront him when he returns from Italy. What is the harm? Why not clear things up, one way or another?"

"You're right. I'm chicken. If I ask, I may find the truth and become disillusioned to find Chris isn't the person I perceived."

"What?" Kate chuckled, "You've already made your mind."

They both laughed at the absurdity.

"Do you want to end up an old maid, curled up in a library as a hopeless wonk? Take charge, and if he is a cad and wants you as a mistress, you must force yourself to move on. You deserve more."

"You're right," Shelby admitted with gusto.

"Now, Kate," Shelby facetiously asked, "what is a hopeless wonk?"

Their laughter echoed out into the hall from the principal's office.

In her cottage, Shelby took stock of all that had happened to her in the past few months. She recalled the trial in Washington, the way Jeb Clayton was led away in tears after the sentencing and shaking while looking back at her. She thought about his remorse and mental suffering and thoughtfully called the detention center for an update. To her surprise, Jeb answered the phone. He explained the counselor recommended him for administrative duties as part of his schooling activities. Her call gave him enormous joy. He sounded almost giddy, telling her how much he enjoyed the opportunity for an education, and that his grades were all good.

"Jeb, that's wonderful. I am so proud of you."

He told her of the creative writing courses included in his curriculum, his advancement toward receiving a high-school diploma, and his desire for college.

"Ms. Evans, I found I enjoy school and learning. When I get my diploma, I am going to apply for a grant to go to college."

"Fine, Jeb," she said, "I will support you every step of the way."

She told him a little about what she writes for the paper and the journalism class at the high school. She mentioned the little filly at the farm she hoped to name.

At Shelby's request, Jeb handed the phone to one of his counselors.

"Ms. Evans, I can confirm, Jeb is a model student. He is developing into a responsible, caring individual. He is an inspiration to others living here, including our staff. We all enjoy him." she said.

After returning the phone to the table, Shelby tucked her hands behind her head and processed the conversation for several minutes. "Of all the wicked things in the world, we saved one young man from a life of crime," she said aloud. She smiled, encouraged about his future. "What a tragedy for him to have suffered the consequences of the other defendants. His father and brother as role models spiral below acceptable."

The good news from Jeb's counselor slackened Shelby's anxiety. Her psyche had suffered an emotional state of flux over the past months. She stretched out on her sofa, relaxed, and in a fetal position fell fast asleep. Glowing as a glimmer of hope, the beam from a candle contained in a safe receptacle on the sofa table, softly glazed her face before slithering into a pool of melted wax. She remained on her sofa until the first sounds of morning awakened her with a melodious tune from a robin calling its mate and the patter of a jogger's feet, presumably her neighbor from down the street, running alongside her small hound.

Fifty-Four

A week passed before Shelby talked to Chris and learned of his updated itinerary. He told her Jason's part in the movie expected to wrap up, and the two men scheduled to meet upon Chris's arrival in the States from Italy. They prepared to return to the farm within a week or ten days.

She didn't understand why she had offered but agreed to pick them up at the airport and drive them to the farm.

"We decided on a name for the filly," she blurted with the excitement of a schoolgirl.

"That's great, Shelby! What are you going to call her?"

"I am going to call her ***Yukon.*** I read a story about Grand Rapids in Canada. The Capital of Yukon is Whitehorse. I chose several and left the final decision to the students. The process served as a geography lesson for them."

"Shelby, Yukon is a wonderful name, and so clever, so appropriate. You always amaze me. I am so looking forward to seeing you. I miss you terribly."

Despite being perplexed by his attention to her and his upcoming marriage, Chris's voice electrified her. She vigorously ruffled her fingers through her hair to throw his words away and attempted to dispel her prolonging desires.

"Why does he say such things? They would arrive home. Who will arrive home?" She said to the phone.

The next day to her friend, Kate, Shelby said, "How can he express excitement for me when he is bringing a fiancé, or by now, maybe a bride? I am a little naïve about Hollywood people, but this seems over the top."

A long pause, and before Kate answered, Shelby began another topic, "I wasn't happy in a large city before," she said as if deciding a resolve. "I agree with Jason. He told me my heart is here and he's right. Therefore, I plan to focus on my career and people in this county and reaching my goals of increasing the educational desires of young people."

"You are doing an extraordinary job, helping this community grow," Kate said. "How wonderful of you to help Effie settle in the town. She is so happy her children can attend school in the city. Effie is doing well in her job at the yard goods store and gaining pride in her work. She is working on alterations for my family and me.

"I am so happy you are staying, Shelby. I'd sincerely miss you." She hugged Shelby, and they said their goodbyes.

Fifty-Five

For a change of pace, Shelby went to Indiana to visit her parents for the weekend. She planned to take the needed time to reflect on goals and how to accept Chris as a friend.

Subtle signs of spring with warm days amid cold nights revealed seasonal weather changes. Shelby found peace when riding her dear horse, Duffy.

"She is no match against Yukon; still, she is endearing and familiar," Shelby smiled to her mother.

The visit home, taking time to remember her roots, provided the medicine she needed. After her stint in the big city of Chicago and becoming friends with a mysterious family with the magical charm and enchantment of Hollywood, the visit home gave her solace. Shelby convinced herself she needed to get down to earth and returned to what she referred to as practical. She prided in being realistic and deciding she needed some downtime, revisited some of her friends from school. Some had settled where they had grown up, married, and had children. She contacted a couple who, as she had, permanently moved away after having graduated college.

Before leaving for Kentucky, Shelby's Mom realized the turmoil her daughter experienced and spoke words of comfort, giving her advice.

"Always follow your heart, dear; your heart will not fail you. The right direction is in store for your future. Don't jump to conclusions thinking nothing good can happen, it can, and will. There is no armor against fate."

Her mother's words stayed with Shelby. Her Mom, always supportive, played a loving role in Shelby's life with her advisory opinions.

Sunday afternoon Shelby arrived at her home in Kentucky. After unpacking, she instinctively drove to the farm. As usual, Ms. Maude anticipated her visit and had prepared dinner for the two of them. In Chris's and Jason's absence, the two ate in the kitchen together.

"Ms. Maude, you spoil me. I realize what Jason meant when he said you and your cooking enticed him to stay,"Shelby said.

"That Mr. Jason, he is always buttering me up," she laughed, "They will be home soon."

"Yes, I'm going to pick them up at the airstrip," Shelby said.

Ms. Maude reasoned Shelby's voice sounded more collected than previously. She didn't appear stirred up emotionally as before.

Shelby began mumbling as she did more frequently but in a good way. She experienced a calmness entering her body after her visit home.

Ms. Maude glared at her, puzzled, "What are you thinking, dear?"

"About what my mother said to me... she said for me to follow my heart, there is no armor against fate. Jason reminded me my heart is here," she said to Ms. Maude, "I agree, and plan to stay here and work on my career goals.

She remembered her mother saying not to jump to conclusions, and mumbled aloud, "Before I establish a case, I must prove sufficient evidence." He has not given any indication to me what he expects of me is immoral, she thought silently.

Shelby hugged a puzzled Ms. Maude before she abruptly left for the barn for a quick gallop on Yukon. The filly helped her to clear her mind and stay in focus of the present.

"I made a connection with my maternal grandfather," Chris told Jason upon returning to the States, "I failed to endear to him under the circumstances, but I am compassionate toward him. I have mixed emotions about the growth of our relationship. It is unclear to me if he accepts the fact, I am related to him. I don't resemble Maria or him. He is far removed from what I expected. He may have been a tyrant in his younger years, but I see him as a weathered page of an old fable."

"Are you in agreement with Maria? Is he involved with your father's death?" Jason asked.

"I'm not sure, but I doubt it. One of Maria's acquaintances in the Ballet Company told him her child had died at birth, a stillborn. I do know it is what Villella believed. Villella glared at me with a blank expression when he realized I might be his grandson. I'm not confident Villella accepted the fact I am his grandson, or maybe he was troubled with lies told to him to withhold information of my birth. However, right before I readied to leave, I looked into his eyes, and I went away believing he hoped it was true. He has no one. I talked to my family, and we want the truth to surface, regardless. The trial will schedule to take place in Florence.

By the way, how is your mom? Has she decided where she wants to live? I haven't talked to her for some time."

"Well, if the wedding isn't enough to keep her off my back, she has been offered a part in Spielberg's new movie."

"That's good, I guess, what about taking time for the honey-moon? Chris asked.

"Don't you remember? She has priorities", they both laughed.

"Her part in the movie calls for an aging film star who cannot accept her role in society," Jason said with a smile, "and she hasn't agreed to play the part," they both laughed again.

"What is your thinking? Will she accept the part?" Chris asked.

"I hope so; it will help keep her out of my business. I love my mom, but she is obstinate. The wedding preparation, on the other hand, is taking all her time at present. The preparation is nothing short of production of a stereotyped Hollywood performance of stars if they all show. I look for her to wait until after the wedding to decide whether or not to accept the part."

Chris raised his eyebrows and smiled, understanding at what his young friend was up against.

"Shelby is picking us up at the airport," Chris said. "I'm anxious to see her, but I suspect she is troubled. I plan to find out wh."

"Maybe all the trauma has caught up with her. I've been worried as well," said Jason.

Fifty-Seven

The days and hours had passed slowly for Chris's while he waited for his return to the States. After he reached California and made plans with Jason, he confirmed flight information to Kentucky by text to Shelby. The private plane, a twin-engine Honda business jet from California scheduled to land in Kentucky at exactly 3:00 pm the next day. Shelby concentrated on her joy to reunite with Jason, but she contrasted her thinking by continually changing outfits. She restyled her hair in several ways until finally, satisfied by what look she wanted.

"Why am I doing this?" she said to her mirror. She denied her goal was to impress Chris but knew otherwise. Unsettled with her contradicting thoughts, she drove to the farm and went directly to the stable and saddled Yukon. She galloped the horse through the meadow at a rapid pace as if it were her last run. Her hair flew in the wind, and her body tensed with anxiety. After reaching quieter tranquility, she slowed the horse and led her to the peaceful lake to drink. She slid from the saddle, breathed deeply of fresh air, and quenched for water, retrieved a bottle from the saddlebag. She sat on a log and began to take deep breaths to relax. She pondered over Chris's homecoming and practiced what she would say to him if he determined to affect her life in any way but above reproach. The words of her mother followed her. ***Follow your heart, no armor against fate.*** An hour later, she sat upon Yukon with a new approach to whatever was to happen and trotted the little Filly, at a slow gait, across the meadow and back to the barn. Ms. Maude waited for her to groom the horse and called her in for dinner.

"I didn't know you knew I was here," she said to Ms. Maude.

"I have many eyes," Ms. Maude told her, "Now, come and eat!"

Shelby went home in the evening before dark and processed her thoughts of how she would react to Chris and Lana. She had no idea of knowing if they were married yet. She tossed and turned like a wild pig during the night, thinking of Chris pursuing her with words and gifts. What was he thinking? Thoughts of infidelity and dishonor bounced around in her head, vying for attention away from positive vibes from her mother.

"Always follow your heart, dear, your heart will not fail you. The right direction is in store for your future. Don't jump to conclusions thinking nothing good can happen, it can and will."

Sun peeked through a fold in the curtains when Shelby awakened in the late morning to the awareness of her aching body from the restless night. Her recollection of nightmares of a sordid affair through the night was of no comfort. Questions remained, and regardless of what takes place, she planned to go about her day as usual until time to head to the airport. Unwelcome butterflies in her stomach offered no help. She quickly ate breakfast, took inventory of what she had planned to wear, showered, styled her hair the way she had in mind to flatter her face, and set out for the farm. Ms. Maud's friendly smile and warm welcome was always a comfort to her.

Shelby glared at the sky from inside the terminal. Her body trembled as the plane cut through the clouds, circled and glided toward the landing strip on the first approach. Shelby's anxiety had grown each hour while she waited for Chris and Jason to arrive. Who would arrive? The big question was, was Lana coming with them? The time was four minutes until three when the wheels quickly touched down, and the plane slowly taxied toward the terminal and rested on its landing gear. After a few minutes, the steps lowered, Jason rushed down and toward Shelby. He gave her a giant hug while Chris waited, a smile on his face. The ring from his aunt was tucked away in his hidden pocket. The incomparable Carlina failed to deplane, a pleasant revelation to Shelby. They had arrived without her.

Chris gently kissed her cheek and firmly held her hand until they reached the car. She marveled at how his eyes sparkled against his sun-tanned face. Her heart began to beat rapidly at the closeness of his body. She prayed he wouldn't feel her trembling arms.

Jason put the bags in the trunk and sat in the rear seat as Shelby drove, sitting next to Chris. The three of them engaged in casual conversation as they drove to the farm. Shelby dared not ask about Lana.

After dinner, prepared by an overjoyed housekeeper who had her family all home at once, the three of them sat casually engaging in small talk. Shelby, feeling a bit uncomfortable, made her apologies, and prepared to go to her cottage. Chris walked her out.

"Shelby, I look forward to seeing you soon. Will you ride with me on Sunday?" he asked, "I want to discuss an important matter with you."

She hesitated before responding. Oh! Oh! What is he going to say? She wondered. I may as well find out, one way or another.

"Yes, I can arrive by seven," she said.

She turned her head to obstruct an advance of which she so yearned. What is this magnetism, this hold he has over me? The question weighed enormously on her mind.

Unsettled by Shelby's mannerisms, Chris stared after her. A chilly rain began to drench his lightweight shirt, and then, her truck faded from sight. Disillusioned, he concluded she lacked the interest in him he so desired. His instincts told him she cared for him, but her actions were contrary to the closeness he desperately wanted to share.

"Chris, is anything wrong?" Jason asked when Chris entered the house with a doomed expression.

Chris, in later years, became much more to Jason than a mentor. They frequently confided in each other as brothers or close friends. However, Chris had not told Jason of any plan to further a relationship with Shelby. It wasn't necessary. The expression well informed Jason on Chris's face as to how far he anticipated the relationship to reach.

"Shelby looks at me with affection, but her responses turn another corner," Chris said to Jason. "She may suffer from depression or working too much or worse. She may be ill. I don't understand what is going on with her."

"I am concerned as well," Jason said, "I will confront her with a brotherly talk."

The two men sat down to relax and discussed Chris's business in Italy and Moscow.

"Wow!" Jason exclaimed when Chris explained his visit with Villella: the accusations; the threats against the witnesses; the devastation over the condition of Giovanni's body when recovered; and triumph after obtaining one piece of crucial evidence saved for over thirty years.

"What is your feeling toward your grandfather now? Will he be exonerated?" Jason asked.

"I believe he will. The evidence showed a person called Alexi Trudeau planned to set my grandfather up as having murdered my father in the event accidental drowning is disproven. Trudeau put together a carefully planned scheme which might have worked had we not become involved. We'll know more when Jack Cravens calls. The informants may have more of an incentive, to tell the truth about what they witnessed when protected by higher courts. Then, too, with the passing of time, major players, the people who threatened them, are either no longer alive or no longer in power for one reason or another.

"Chris, I must say, the outcome all comes down to your determination and dedication to your father's memory," Your father would be proud, as well as Maria. I'm proud of you."

The two briefly embraced and said goodnight. Jason went directly to the phone to call Shelby before the late hour and invited her to breakfast with him the next morning.

"I need help on an urgent matter and want your advice, he told her.

"Of course, Jason, I'm happy to help any way I can," she said, assuming he

referred to himself and Sunni. "I will see you tomorrow."

She slept peacefully during the night, drained of all emotions that dominated her existence: excitement, fear, joy, grief, love, and regretfully, lust.

The next morning, Shelby and Jason exchanged small talk over coffee at the local diner, when he abruptly got right to the point, or nearly.

Fifty-Eight

"Shelby, a friend of mine who is enamored with a young lady, needs help. His affection for a young lady is obvious. By the way, she looks at him; it doesn't take a team of soothsayers to grasp her affection for him. The problem is, she shuns away when he gets close. She sometimes comes off a little bitter and says things were failing to make sense. What is your intake about such a problem?"

"Jason, what on earth are you talking about?"

"Chris, I am talking about you and Chris," he said lovingly.

"Jason, what is it you and Chris expect from me?

"What do you mean? We want you to be yourself and happy, nothing more. If you are ill or depressed, we love you and want to help.

"Please, tell me what is wrong," he asked.

"Chris is betrothed or married to your mother, and he makes advances toward me.

"WHAT"? Jason yelled. He sat back in the chair so surprised; he was speechless. And then, his laughter rumbled through the restaurant and out to the sidewalk. "Is that all it is?"

Shelby saw no humor in what she had told him. She responded with what sounded to him like righteous anger.

"Jason, what do you mean, all it is? That pretty much sums it up."

He choked back another laugh, caught his breath and took her hands to calm her down blurted out

"Lana is already married," he said calmly, with a fixed grin on his face. She married Christopher last week but not our Christopher. Chris was in Italy and couldn't attend the wedding. She married Christopher Conliffe, a producer who pursued her for years. The elaborate Hollywood wedding went as planned, and they are on their honeymoon in Hawaii. A romantic relationship between Lana and Chris never existed. Lana gives false impressions because of her jealousy. She appointed herself as the single capable person to choose a bride for either Chris or me, which we usually ignore. She considers us her property."

"But Ms. Maude brought a magazine home, which described Christopher Stone as her fiancée," she declared.

"I should've suspected, Ms. Maude found the "rag" magazine with the false story. The editor retracted the mistake immediately. Chris ignores the tabloids. Stories of this nature with no credibility happens a lot in Hollywood by so-called journalists.

Jason started laughing again, "Lana and Chris?" he laughed and shook his head side to side in disbelief.

Shelby picked up a menu and started hitting him, "Why didn't you tell me? Ms. Maude expected he planned to bring Lana to the farm as his bride," she said.

"My dear Shelby, Lana is my mother, but even I would be upset if that happened. Chris has been eating his heart out for you ever since he started working again in California and before going to Italy on this recent trip. Chris assumed you felt the same. The ball is in your court now," he chuckled, not being able to contain himself.

"We suspected you suffered from an illness or depression," he explained, "This is fixable."

"Jason, I've been so wrong. How can I fix it?" she asked him, tears in her eyes.

"Go with your guard down. Keep your date to ride with him," he said. "Follow your heart."

He started talking like her mom, she thought.

She gave him a quick hug, and after he left, still chuckling, she went home where she removed her helmet and saddle from the shipping box and gave each a kiss.

The sun brightly engulfed the Standish property, like a supportable peacock, when Shelby arrived early Sunday morning. Shelby found Ms. Maude was waiting for her with arms outstretched.

"Shelby, Love, Mr. Chris, did not marry Ms. Lana. I am so happy," he said we are mad to favor such a notion."

"I found out, Ms. Maude. We made assumptions by a misprint."

The two women embraced with tears in their eyes. Chris came up from behind and hugged them both.

"Shelby, how did you not realize my love for you, my furtive glances, and innuendoes on the phone? he scolded after backing away. "You must have known. What were you thinking, I would marry someone else and keep you as a pet?"

They both laughed at the absurdity.

"Of course, I knew," she teased.

He beckoned his hand and took her into his arms, eliminating any doubt. Their eyes met, and Shelby vowed not to turn from him again. She promised to, in the future, to leave the tabloid reading exclusively to Ms. Maude.

As for Ms. Maude's reaction to the union between the two people she loved like family, the word 'delighted' paled compared to her having had bought the choicest piece of land in the world.

The following weekend they were seated at a dinner party Chris had arranged at the farm in honor of their union as a couple. Shelby and Chris, Jason, Shelby's parents, the Shoney's, and Kate, along with her husband, were having dessert when Ms. Maude called Shelby to the phone.

"Ms. Shelby, come quick. Someone from Sotheby's in New York is on the phone. He wants to talk to you about your art."

When she returned to the table, her face was white.

"Shelby, dear, what is wrong?" asked Chris. Everyone sat, mouths open, not breathing.

Shelby started to tear, and then she blurted out, "A painting of mine sold at auction in New York for a large sum. I think I shall faint," she said, pressing the palm of her hand upon her forehead. "I had no idea when I signed permission for the painting to go to auction it would ever amount to anything. That's why I didn't say anything. My mom was the only person who knew."

"What? What painting?" they asked. Everyone waited. Chris brought out the champagne before Shelby said anything. Everyone stood, toasted Shelby's success cheered, and sang praises while they waited to hear about the painting.

"Wow! Shelby," Jason said. "I'm not the least surprised. I told you your art was magnificent."

"It was a painting of myself, dirty and scruffy, sitting upon a log at the lake surrounded by trees. I painted how I saw myself before I found the farm. It was the image of myself when I first met Chris, she said, catching his proud and sympathetic smile. I painted the incredible landscape and Yukon grazing nearby. I didn't believe I had given the scenery justice, but someone thought so.

"Dear Shelby," Chris said as he took her in his arms. "You must have put enormous feeling into that piece." And then everyone laughed when he said he wished he had outbid the buyer.

"And Sam, don't be looking for a replacement for me anytime soon," Shelby said, creating laughter.

Later, Sam printed a special edition in his newspaper featuring his young assistant. He had located a photograph of the painting, sold to an anonymous connoisseur of art, published in the newspapers alongside Shelby's biography. Critics celebrated the canvas by their reviews of praise. A London critic described how the painting held a sense of strength and survival that only the artist could have experienced. Clouds of angels high above the water depicted immortality with atmospheric mystery. The painting, delivered to the private home of an aristocrat in London, England, and overnight, Shelby had reached National acclaim in the world of art.

When Chris studied the painting, he marveled at the emotional intensity of which he knew all too well. It was one of the reasons he had become so drawn to and enamored by the woman whom he intended for his bride.

During the following weeks, Chris endeavored to begin a formal courtship with Shelby. They frequently rode together, enjoyed dinner dates by candlelight at the farm, and on other occasions, they flew to nearby cities for formal outings. On her twenty-eighth birthday, Chris chartered a flight to take them to the Florida Keys. From there, they traveled by boat to a remote tropical island, away from paparazzi, where he had reserved a restaurant, complete with a small orchestra, for the two of them. Before dinner, as the music played softly, Chris got down on one knee and presented her with his grandmother's ring. Shelby was speechless.

"Shelby, I waited for you all my life. Will you make me the happiest man on earth and marry me?"

Shelby was in awe of such a surprise. She hadn't expected a proposal so soon. She told him later she wondered why they were alone in the restaurant and wondered when other guests would arrive. Shelby had begun to worry; maybe it wasn't a popular spot. She hadn't suspected he paid for the entire restaurant.

"Chris, this ring is magnificent. The brilliance and beauty of such an outstanding ring are incredible. I am speechless, and the fact it belonged to your Grandmother makes it doubly special. I will cherish it forever."

"Does that mean your answer is yes?"

"Yes! Yes! Yes!" she cried with joy.

"Good, now can I get up off my knees? She laughed as he rose to his feet, took her into his arms, professed his love, and sealed the affirmation with a lingering kiss as the orchestra played a celebration tune.

"I will love you forever," she whispered.

"Forever is how long we will be together," he said lovingly," They held their embrace for several seconds after which they drank a toast to their future and danced while the orchestra played a medley of love songs. The couple's happiness swept over everyone close to them, and after their engagement, they rarely separated.

Fifty-Nine

After Cravens informed Chris of the trial date in Florence, Chris brought Shelby up to date on recent business in Italy, of his reconnection with the Sforza's, and about Maria's father, his grandfather living in Moscow. Chris also explained how his grandfather was a suspect in the death of his father.

"The trial scheduled to take place in Florence," he said.

Shelby absorbed the tribulations Chris had suffered from compassion. She had little previous knowledge of his business or personal affairs, only what she had read in conducting a private search, which she planned to keep to herself, at least for the time being.

Jason traveled to California to visit with Sunni and prepare for the premiere of their movie. At the same time, Chris worked out of the Mayor's office, reviewing government contracts, donations, and other issues where he had become involved to improve the town. Shelby resumed her work at the newspaper and dedicated time to the children in her journalism class.

When the movie in which Jason and Sunni starred, ***Distinguished Voice,*** scheduled to premiere in Hollywood, Chris, Shelby, and Ms. Maude attended, along with Lana and her new husband, whom she introduced to everyone at a dinner before the celebration. Shelby marveled at how cordial and pleasant Lana had become since her marriage to Christopher Conliffe.

After the premiere celebration and reviewing the comments by those in attendance, everyone waited for critic reviews—good Fortune for everyone. The Morning headlines praised the actors and the film.

A few weeks after their return from California, Chris received a call from Cravens. A date for the trial in Florence of those implicated in the killing of Sforza scheduled to begin.

"Also," Cravens informed Chris, "After what we discovered during the intensive investigation, your grandfather was not likely involved. We have concluded he was singled out and victimized as well. It appears Trudeau framed him to ward off suspicion toward others as we had surmised."

"That is good news! Thank you, Jack."

"We can all thank the people who decided to come forward with condemning information hidden for years. They are all committed to telling the truth."

"What about responsibility, the primary suspect? Has he been identified?" asked Chris.

"A Russian Oligarch is the prime suspect and indicted for several felonies. He became obsessed with Maria's talent and beauty. The Russian couldn't bear the thought of Maria with anyone but him, although, according to her peers, she paid little attention to him and shied away from his advances. He was an essential contributor to the Ballet Company and arrogant enough to claim ownership of the cast.

"Good work! I'll prepare to leave for Florene soon."

Chris relayed his discussion with Jack to Shelby, Maude, and Jason before preparing for his trip. He invited Shelby along, but she declined, thinking it not a good idea to put another burden upon him by looking after her. Since their engagement, he had become particularly attentive toward her.

Sixty

When he arrived in Florence, Chris, his cousins, Cravens, and Guinizelli went over their findings, along with Boulud, before the day of the trial.

The trial lasted seven days before going to the jury. All three informants identified as having close connections to police officials at the time of the murder. Each gave damning testimony against the excused. A woman, Pia St. Vincent, who had worked close to the now-retired department head at the police station, gave a condemning account against the former Police Chief. She had overheard conversations and read documents outlining a conspiracy plot implicating the, now aged Italian Police Chief, and others on trial. Her coworkers in whom she confided, backed her story.

Villella and Chris exchanged polite glances as they caught sight of each other in the courtroom. Instead of for the defense, Villella sat as a subpoenaed witness for the prosecution. When on the stand, he pointed the finger at Alexi Trudeau, a Frenchman who brought false information to him about his daughter and her child. Two informants identified Trudeau as the person who introduced himself as Villella and planned for a courier to bring money to dispose of the target, describing Giovanni Sforza as the target. The imposter, posing as Villella, supplied the policeman with information of

Sforza's work habits, which Pia St. Vincent, admitted she read. St. Vincent was present when the monies exchanged, but kept quiet, afraid for her life. Another informant testified he witnessed the chief knock Sforza unconscious with, "what Americans call, a Billy Club, and put him in the rear seat of an unmarked police vehicle." The evidence followed the money transfer from a Russian Oligarch, Igor Korsakov, to Trudeau. Trudeau, a known criminal, and hitman later identified as one of Korsakov's henchmen implicated Korsakov as having ordered and paid for the hit. It was no accident for Trudeau to have hidden a paper in Villella's apartment. He purposely left the note with the victim's name to implicate Villella if officers visited Villella's home. Korsakov, described as having unmatched greed for wealth, acquired an absolute passion for the Ballet, and a sensual appetite for the star, Maria Villella. When he became aware of Maria's involvement with a fisherman, his depraved desires gave way to relentless cruelty. After the defendants were pronounced guilty, Korsakov raised his arms in defiance, yelled obscenities in his native language, and was dragged out of the courtroom by two policemen. The informants previously threatened, came forward, giving their account of finding Sforza's body, and were exonerated. All defendants involved in the killing received life sentences, including the surviving police who were involved.

The Sforza family celebrated in high spirits. They praised Christopher, whose goal to find truth led to rejuvenating a case, wrongfully classified as accidental. Stone's efforts ultimately proved the murder of his father. The greed of money and the covetous desires of a rapacious pirate had resulted in his father's unmercifully death.

After the courtroom emptied, Chris said to his family of Richard Villella, "I'm happy he was proven innocent of any involvement."

When Stone searched for his grandfather, he found Villella had vanished along with the spectators. He called for Cravens, and the two of them began looking for the older man. Cravens got in touch with his magical powers as an investigator and reached the driver who took Villella to the airport. He and Chris searched the waiting area in the loading zone at the airport until they came upon an exhausted older adult, solemnly slumped in a wheelchair and waiting at the gate, ready to board his flight to Moscow. When Chris reached him, the older man's grimness faded. His face brightened with a broad smile. This stranger, whom he had recently found, his grandson, went to the trouble to come to him. Chris shook his hand and escorted him onto the plane, making sure he was comfortable. His grandfather grinned with tears in his eyes as he watched Chris walk away from the plane, waving. Grandfather and Grandson, at last, connected as a family.

Sixty-One

Chris and Shelby decided upon a June wedding. They planned to have an intimate ceremony at the farm, inviting friends and neighbors whom they had gotten to know and respect in their community. However, the list began to grow.

Shelby shopped with her mother for a simple but classic wedding gown and chose a unique design from a known designer.

Ms. Maude, with the aid of professional staff, transformed the Standish estate into an elegant setting fit for royalty, including fresh flowers throughout the house. The kitchen converted into a productive work area accommodating the chefs and kitchen crew, preparing an elaborate feast to serve at the reception.

Chris's cousins arrived with their families, including Aunt Gina. Aunt Gina graciously accepted to substitute for Chris's mother. She brought along an elegant lavender gown of Italian lace to wear at the wedding.

"Maria had told me it was her favorite color," she told Shelby. The two of them

found they had much to talk about since they both were accomplished artists.

Chris sent an invitation to his grandfather with a generous check inside, plus an airline ticket. The older man accepted but had not arrived.

On the day of the wedding, a gentle breeze floated over the guests under a sky, blue as an inlet of the Tyrrhenian Sea. A proud moment for Shelby's Mom, who looked nearly as young as her daughter. Her elegant, ankle-length gown of pale-yellow chiffon complemented her petite figure and golden hair.

Those who lived in the county had never witnessed Christopher Standish without the wig. Chris's neighbors and Kentucky friends were in awe at his appearance. Chris dressed in a white tuxedo and white patent shoes, as did the best man, Jason, and Shelby's father. The white satin bow tie set Chris apart from his best man and future father-in-law, whose bow ties were of celery green.

Kate, the matron of honor, walked down the aisle with refined grace. She wowed the crowd of students in an ankle-length gown the color of raw celery, complimenting her African American skin. Ms. Maude, honored as a family member, fashionably dressed in an elegant long gown of robin egg blue.

Music, at Shelby's request, featured the local high-school orchestra. Effie's' two children, as flower girls, dressed in delicate pink chiffon were a crowd-pleaser. The little girls in A-line, floor-length dresses with Bateau necklines dropped rose petals along the white covered path.

Shelby, radiantly glowed, holding a lush bouquet of white orchids while escorted by her father. Her delicate, white gossamer gown with a strapless bodice and full, ankle-length skirt embroidered with cascading white poppies presented a subtle dimensional effect—a classic without ostentatious detail. She looked stunning in an elegant sheer veil of delicate lace, tipped at the shoulders, and circled a crown of jewels. The veil barely covered her face. Her white satin pumps complimented slender ankles.

As Shelby walked gracefully toward her groom, she mirrored him as her image of a dashing Italian or Grecian Prince

'Married to the girl of my dreams at last,' thought Christopher Stone. 'Life doesn't get better.'

Lana, her new husband, Christopher, along with Shelby's boss, Sam, and his wife, Betty, mingled among the guests. Locals who attended included town officials, Chief Jeffries, his wife, and off-duty deputies. Judge Morley, Kate's husband, officiated the ceremony. Also, Mr. & Mrs. Beasley attended, along with Jack Cravens and his wife.

Shelby's entire journalism class was among the guests, and Sam had offered each an assignment to cover the wedding as a surprise for their teacher, the bride.

A gala affair, indeed, and first of its kind in one small town in Kentucky. Private planes graced the local airstrip and delivered Hollywood celebrities who filled Jerimiah's Lodge with affluence.

Shelby's dad, John, walked Shelby through an isle of perfectly trimmed evergreens, upstaged by exquisite white orchids, and interspersed with luxurious white roses and rose geraniums. The setting mirrored one equal to a celebratory Hollywood event, according to the gossip columnists. The local newspaper proudly boasted a guest list of four hundred friends and townspeople. Once word spread through tabloids, paparazzi determined to get exclusive pictures with a high-powered lens. They perched on tops of barns, hid in the underbrush, and sat hovered inside helicopters over vacant meadows.

Gifts from the Best Man included catering by a celebrity chef whose staff arrived early to enlist help from local cooks and servers in preparation and to prepare the delicacies Jason requested.

Bonnie's bakery brought a monstrous Italian cream wedding cake and smaller cupcakes elegantly decorated with white, pink, and pale-yellow rosebuds.

White tablecloths, place settings of bone china, exquisite silverware, candles, and orchids adorned over 150 tables on the west lawn to accommodate the guests for a sit-down dinner.

Sixty-Two

After the wedding excitement died away, Ms. Maude vacationed in London, while Chris and Shelby spent their honeymoon in the south of France.

Upon returning from their honeymoon, Chris surprised Shelby with another gift.

"Now close your eyes and take my hand." She obeyed, and he led her to an elevator reaching the top floor of their home, which she had thought of as an attic. She stepped off the elevator and walked into what she imagined as a lovely penthouse. Her eyes had opened to a beautiful art studio, complete with supplies she used for her paintings. The walls, painted with sky blues and pale yellows, shone with a splendor of open seas. There were large windows through which to view the earth and where the sky met the horizon. Mountaintops stood quietly in the distance, under rounded heaps of moving clouds. Skylights furnished the room with additional light. Easels, placed in strategic positions where the sun shone from behind and above, held proper canvas ready to paint. Chris had ordered art supplies recommended by a noted gallery entrepreneur and had them delivered.

Shelby stood silent for a long time before turning toward him with tears flowing down her cheeks. He then took her hand for the grand tour.

A comfortable lounge with all the amenities embraced an area in which to rest or meet with clients. A wet bar stocked favorite household wines and, of course, cognac. A fully equipped bath and bedroom occupied the far end.

"How, on earth, did you pull this off without my knowledge? I'm supposed to be a nosy reporter. The studio is the most beautiful studio I could have ever imagined."

"This was all put together while we were away," he said, holding her close.

"This is so beautiful; I don't want to leave," she said. And they didn't. At least not until morning.

Chris served the two of them champagne and hors d'oeuvres. It was the next morning before they entered the elevator wrapped in white bathrobes. Days later, while Shelby busied in the studio organizing her paints and supplies, Chris received an urgent message from someone in Russia, an acquaintance of his grandfather. Villella had become gravely ill, and in desperation, the friend, a neighbor named Otto, called Chris, remembering he was the older man's only known relative. He had found Chris's information in Villella's belongings.

Chris responded immediately. He realized the reason Villella did not show up for his wedding and made plans to return to Moscow.

Upon arriving at the Sheremetyevo International, Chris contacted Norty, the driver he used on his previous trip, who was, fortunately, available and promptly drove to the airport. When Chris and Norty arrived at the address Otto had given him, Chris found his grandfather in an unsuitable home for the aged. The retirement or nursing home was in dreadful need of repair, and thinking of his animals, Chris decided, not sanitary enough for a barn. The facility was as dark and dreary as an unused dirt cellar. Pungent odors of bodily fluids ranked in the hallways, and the stench of death lingered from the night before. The room, in which his grandfather shared with three others, groaned in despair. The older man smiled through a sore and bruised mouth and extended his arm when Chris entered the room. His bloodshot eyes began to tear. His clothes were dirty, his hair long and tangled, and his beard unshaven for days, maybe weeks.

"So, this is why you didn't show up for my wedding, flimsy excuse," Chris kidded. Chris's grandfather suffered from malnutrition, bedsores, neglect, and abuse. Chris contacted his grandfather's friend, Otto, and with his help along with help from Norty, as an interpreter, decided for his grandfather to go immediately to a hospital where he abled to monitor his grandfather's care. Chris, then, called his new wife and told her of his plan to bring Villella to Kentucky. She embraced the idea and suggested Chris stay in Moscow until his grandfather's health had improved enough for him to travel.

It took some doing, but with Chris's influence and contacts to the right people, he obtained an extended visa for his grandfather to remain in the United States throughout the rest of his life. When he told his grandfather, he was going home with him; the older man became teary-eyed. However, due to his injuries caused by abuse in the nursing home, and his present health condition, he would have to wait for several days to travel, even in a hospital equipped plane. Chris stayed in Moscow for another two weeks, making sure his grandfather received the treatment he needed and given respect all patients deserve. When confident the old man had gained enough strength for the trip, they left for the United States on a medical flight with a physician and two nurses.

Epilogue

Christopher Stone, a contributor and supporter of the community in which he lived, and supporter of the State of Kentucky, purchased land inside the city limits of his county and constructed a zoological garden gifted to the town from both him and his wife who orchestrated the project. His wife named it "Noah's Place". The impressive garden and facility included a veterinarian, a zoologist, and a team of caretakers. People of all ages influenced by the study of animals and animal life often frequented the garden. The center became part of the agenda for classrooms in surrounding cities. Also, the Stones donated additional funds to the high school, developing a theater arts program, Chris's idea.

Sheriff Jeffries expanded his department after housing developers began constructing subdivisions, inviting families to the area. Additional shops and streetlights became a necessity. Sam Shoney expanded the newspaper staff. Jeb Clayton, with outstanding high-school credits, entered college through an anonymous scholarship program where he excelled in journalism. After college, he became an apprentice for Sam Shoney and was later promoted as a replacement for Shelby Stone after the townspeople elected her Mayor. The future of Poa continually expanded in growth, offering opportunities abounded for success and prosperity. Shelby's paintings had become recognized in the world of art and quite lucrative. She continued to paint in her spare time and began painting portraits after having been commissioned by Carlina.

"Who knew?"

General knowledge of the expanding community began to spread and gain National acclaim for its achievements. Christopher Stone, producer and screenwriter, elected to join political adventures but declined to run for Governorship of Kentucky. Stone frequently traveled to Hollywood for production assignments, and when her schedule permitted, accompanied by his wife.

Jason, when on Holiday from increasing demands from Hollywood, frequently returned with his family to the solitude and friendship of his Kentucky family. His wife, Sunni, retired from the movie industry and became a full-time mother to their twin boys, Christopher, and Giovanni.

Ms. Maude remained a faithful servant, and more as a friend, confidant, and family member. She, along with Shelby and Chris, glorified to have the twins on whom to dote. As for Lana Carlina-Conliffe and her husband, they traveled abroad frequently and surprisingly visited the farm on occasion. Carlina's attitude had remarkably improved. Shelby credited the change to Carlina's new husband, a kind, understanding individual with lots of patience, bringing forth the attention and happiness she craved.

However, an article printed in a tabloid emphasized how the bride at a small-town wedding in Kentucky to a famous Hollywood celebrity had upstaged Lana Carlina, a famous movie star who attended as a guest. Lana soon became known in the film industry as a former beauty queen, retired actress, and, recently, as Jason Vance's mother.

The little filly, Yukon, well, she became in foal the next spring, along with her owner, the Mayor of Poa.

As for Richard Villella, the aging gentleman from Moscow delighted in having a relationship with his grandson, who arranged a suite of rooms at the farm for the old gentleman's comfort. Villella enjoyed having the portrait of his beloved daughter, Maria, in his spacious living area. Ms. Maude coddled him out of depression and sickness while Shelby and Chris lovingly watched the friendship between the two develop into more of a contented partnership. Chris's grandfather and Ms. Maude often shared a taste of Brandy in the evenings and sometimes sipped the forever house favorite, a fine bottle of cognac.

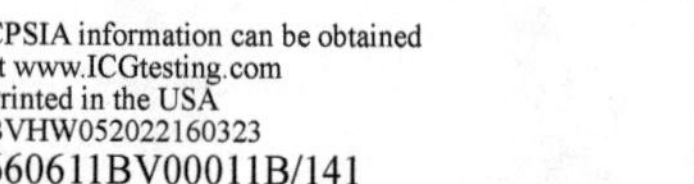

CPSIA information can be obtained
at www.ICGtesting.com
Printed in the USA
BVHW052022160323
660611BV00011B/141

9 781662 873126